THE RENEGADE GIRLS TINKERING CLUB

RENEGADE STYLE

Terri Selting David

To Mom, who was totally right.

And also to caffeine, which is often totally right as well.

A PERFECT OPPORTUNITY

*a*mber Rosenberg finished the application with a flourish, using her purple glitter pen to dot the last "i" with a heart. She carefully turned it over and re-read the flier on the other side.

Do you:
Love making high quality custom clothes?
Have your own unique style?
Want to learn about the business of fashion?
Are you the best at what you do?*

BESPOKE CUSTOM CLOTHIERS' new **YOUTH INTERNSHIP** *Position might be the perfect opportunity for you!*

Can YOU make the cut?

Five applicants will compete in a Fashion Face-Off to showcase their own custom designed and created fashion collection. **GRADES 6-12 ELIGIBLE**.

To apply, fill out the application on the back of this flier and return to the INTERNSHIP box in the store.

This was it. The perfect chance to show the world what Amber Rosenberg was made of. The perfect opportunity to really BE somebody. Bespoke was her favorite fashion boutique, full of the most amazing handmade, custom clothing ever. She wasn't sure what exactly a youth internship was, but she knew she wanted to be a part of it.

Clothes littered the dusty pink bedspread behind her, draped over mounds of furry pillows. Flowing blouses, sundresses in delicate pastel blues and spring greens, dark stretchy leggings with rhinestones on the cuffs. Even a pantsuit with knotted shoulders. A smattering of finely crafted and expensive clothes mingled with swarms of the latest mall fashion.

And then there were the clothes she'd made herself. Amber loved to make all kinds of things but sewing was her favorite. Finding beautiful fabrics, then carefully cutting and piecing them together to create a whole new outfit from a pattern, picture, or even her imagination made her feel powerful. Special. With her sewing skills, a little practice, and some help from Granny, any clothes she wanted could be hers to wear, and they'd fit her perfectly. Anything she saw or designed or dreamt could come to life under her sewing machine's presser foot.

One of her own creations lay across the bed, too. A sleeveless dress with wide shoulder straps and a handkerchief hem. The turquoise cotton fabric was soft and the asymmetrical skirt hung to just below the knees, swooshing pleasantly.

It wasn't bad. But was it special enough for today?

Was she the best at what she did? Well, she was only eleven. But she'd practiced long enough and made enough mistakes in all the years she'd been sewing that she was pretty good at it by now — now that she was in sixth grade. And grades six through twelve were eligible for the internship. SHE was eligible.

Amber had gone to Ada Lovelace Charter School, in the middle of San Francisco, since first grade. Lovelace went from kindergarten all the way through eighth grade before feeding into Babbage High School. The transition to the upper floors that housed the middle school was more than just another flight of steps, though. It was a whole new experience.

Sixth grade had started out with a bang. She'd made friends with some of the most popular kids in school: Benjamin Spencer, president of the student council, and Gail Mendez, head of the school newspaper. They were both in eighth grade. Together, along with her best friends in the Renegade Girls Tinkering Club, they'd even solved a crime.

Digging into her stuffed closet, Amber tossed a lilac designer dress onto a nearby chair. Its full skirt drifted down like clouds around the chair's plush peacock velvet.

It was perfect. A dress that would really get people's attention. She pulled it over her head and slipped into her favorite blue sequin-toed flats. Their purpley-blue color was an unusual choice with lilac, a bold fashion choice that was perfect for today. The shoes barely fit anymore, but she loved them too much to let go. She grabbed a necklace with a pendant the same blue as the shoes to tie the outfit together.

Now for the finishing touch.

A white plastic package waited on the bed. Amber gazed proudly at the international mailing label, then ripped open the packaging and dumped out a brand new backpack wrapped in clear cellophane. It glittered from turquoise to purpley-pink across the front. There was nothing wrong with her old backpack, but this one came straight from Italy. Imported, flown halfway across the world. It was super special. She pulled off the crisp, crinkly cellophane and the soft, clear plastic underneath.

She'd be the best dressed kid at school today. Tucking the Bespoke flier tenderly into the front pocket, Amber filled her new backpack with the contents of the old. Then she grabbed her pink furry jacket, pausing to gaze at her reflection in her bedroom mirror. The skirt flared and settled as she did a little spin. She watched her wonderful wavy auburn hair shimmer around her shoulders in the morning sun. Perfect.

The pile of plastic packaging on the bedspread caught her eye.

She imagined her mom's voice scolding, "Where does that go, honey?"

Amber diligently crammed all the plastic into her trash can and rushed down to breakfast.

The smell of bacon and coffee poured out of the kitchen, mixed with a lot of noise. Her brothers.

No one noticed her enter the kitchen. Her younger brother Blaise's backpack almost hit her in the face as he swung it onto his shoulder.

"I don't want to brush my teeth!" he shouted as he stomped past.

"Do it anyway," their mom yelled back, dropping her plate into the sink with a clatter. "Are you wearing underwear?"

"Good morning," Amber said, moving out of his way.

He didn't answer.

Dad sat at the table sipping from a mug, munching on toast and bacon. Next to him, her older brother Aiden sipped from an identical mug with an identical little slurp. Dad wore a finely tailored shirt and silk tie. Aiden wore a burgundy velvet tuxedo jacket with a black satin collar.

Coffee scent wafted from her dad's mug, but as she sat next to her brother, Amber could smell chocolate. Dad poured in some cream and swirled it around. Aiden copied him, watching Blaise storm down the hall.

"That boy is so childish," Aiden sigh as he took another slurp. "I love a good cup of coffee in the morning!"

Amber rolled her eyes. Aiden was just about to turn thirteen, and despite what he told everyone, he didn't seem particularly mature to Amber. "I know it's just chocolate, dumbface. I can smell it."

Aiden ignored her.

Dad grunted and turned to Mom. "I have an early meeting, can you bring the kids to school today?"

Mom sighed, picking up her phone. "Let me see if I can reschedule my call with New York. Aiden, go brush your teeth, too."

"Aw Mom, I'm not a little kid," he whined, sounding very much like a little kid.

"Well did you brush them?" She glared at him over the top of her phone. "And put on more appropriate school clothes, young man! We leave in five minutes."

He grumbled, shoving back his chair and almost tripping over Amber.

"Out of the way, shorty," he barked at her.

"Aiden," Mom snapped as she poked at her phone. "Don't tease your sister."

"Good morning," Amber said brightly. She stood and brushed out her dress, turning around for her mom's approval. "How do I look today?"

"Great, honey," Mom said without looking up. "We leave in five minutes."

Amber sighed and grabbed a granola bar for the road. The flier sat safely in her backpack pocket. She'd show it to her friends today at school. Get them on board to help. None of them were that into fashion, but surely they'd support her, unlike when she ran for student council.

She hadn't told her friends about her candidacy before she'd signed up, just assumed they'd drop everything to help her with her campaign. She hadn't considered their feelings or other commitments. It had been selfish, and she'd almost lost them forever because of it.

But she'd learned her lesson. It was important to get everyone to agree to a big project before she could expect their help. It wasn't fair to make big decisions and expect other people to just go along with them. That wasn't friendship. She knew that now.

Besides, there was no way Amber could compete against twelfth-graders without their help. So this time she'd do it right. She'd talk to them from the very beginning. This time they'd work together.

2

WHAT DOES A SCIENTIST LOOK LIKE?

*M*om's Tesla SUV pulled up to the curb at Ada Lovelace Charter School. The morning sun was bright, but November's chilly air promised colder days ahead. Amber's brothers spilled out before the car even stopped, and disappeared inside the school. Amber, left behind, bolted after them.

Kids streamed into the front doors of Lovelace. So many kids. It was easy to get lost among them all. Hard to stand out. To people who knew her at all, Amber was known as the science kid. The girl with the answers. She even memorized the scientific names of various plants and animals as a little hobby. It wasn't exactly a flashy hobby, but it was a lot of fun, and she was proud of how many genus and species names she'd collected.

Despite the hoards of students swarming around, Lovelace was a lot quieter since the student elections had ended. A few weeks ago, the halls had been lined with obnoxiously bright campaign posters, including her own. Now they were beige again, dotted with random art projects and the occasional inspirational or educational poster. Amber paused in front of one of those posters on the first floor. It told her she was in a Bully Free Zone.

The anti-bullying campaign had been the work of Benjamin and his student council. Down the hall, she suddenly noticed the thrum of kid chatter getting louder. Benjamin himself must have arrived, almost as though she'd summoned him. Saying hi to him, especially when she looked so nice, would be a great start to her morning. She turned towards the sounds. A wave of older kids swarmed through the hall like a tsunami, forcing her back against the wall.

"Benjamin!" she called, waving a hand as high as she could. She could hardly hear her own voice above the chatter. "Hi!"

Benjamin and the other kids swept past, swarming up the stairs to the middle school on the top two floors of the building. Then they were gone. He hadn't even noticed she was there. She sighed.

The hallway seemed a little emptier now. She pushed herself off the wall and smoothed out her dress. Unzipping the pocket of her backpack, she made sure the application was still inside.

Something bumped into her leg.

A little boy looked around nervously, not even aware he'd collided with her. He was obviously in one of the elementary school grades on the bottom three floors. It was hard to imagine she and her friends had been that little, once upon a time.

He looked lost. Tears were forming in his eyes and he sniffled back the snot oozing from his nose. Amber knelt beside him. At his level, all she could see were the older kids' legs. Benjamin's crowd must have terrified him.

"Hey there, you okay?" she asked.

"Where's my classroom? I can't see it," the boy squeaked.

Amber held out a hand. The boy grabbed it tightly as she asked, "Which is your class?"

"Mrs. Armstrong." He rubbed his nose with his free hand, then wiped it off on his pant leg. "Hey. Are you a princess? You look like a princess."

"Thank you." Amber smiled down at her dress. "Can I help you find your classroom? I'm a little early." It was a lie. She might actually be late. But the boy nodded gratefully.

Gliding through the quickly dissipating kids, Amber read the teacher names on each door.

"Here it is," she said finally, gently pushing the boy inside. The hall was almost empty and she didn't want to be late for her own class. It was science, her favorite.

She turned to leave, but before she knew what was happening, the boy dragged her over to a deep windowsill. Little cups full of soil sat proudly in the morning sun. The boy pointed to one with a name that looked like Mitchell scrawled on the side.

"Look!" he beamed. "It's my cherry tree! I planted it

myself. Do you like cherries? It's going to be a whole tree. You can have some cherries tomorrow."

"Cherries are my favorite!" Amber smiled. "But cherry trees take a really long time to grow. Did you know the scientific name for a cherry tree is *prunus*? You probably have a *prunus avium* there, a sweet cherry."

"Wait," Mitchell looked confused. "Are you a princess or a scientist? You don't look like a scientist."

Amber frowned, looking down at her dress again. "What does a scientist look like? I love science, especially biology..."

A bell rang.

"CRAP!" Amber yelled.

The entire first-grade classroom, suddenly silent, stared at her in shock. Mrs. Armstrong scowled.

"Sorry!" she blushed. "I meant darn it! I mean, I'm late! Gotta go."

She slid out the door and raced up the stairs, her sparkling flats flapping off her heels. They were shoes made for dancing or standing around looking fabulous. Running was too much to ask of them.

Gasping for breath, she reached her fourth-floor locker and shoved in her backpack. Hurriedly tugging out her science books and slamming the door shut, she started down the hall to class.

The door popped back open. The lockers at Lovelace didn't have locks.

Groaning, she doubled back and kicked the door shut with one floppy shoe. Then she realized she was still wearing her furry jacket. The locker slammed shut a third time with the jacket inside and thankfully stayed shut.

Finally flopping into her seat next to her best friend, Wren Sterling, Amber reached for the flier. Which she'd accidentally left in her locker.

Her perfect day was already starting to unravel.

3

UNRAVELING

"*Y*ou look pretty." Wren eyed Amber suspiciously. "You know we're doing a hands-on experiment today, right?"

"We what?" Amber panted. "Oh. Oh yeah. I forgot. Darn it! This morning isn't going at all the way I planned."

"I promise not to fling goop all over your fancy dress," Wren smirked.

Amber looked down at her dress. At least Wren had noticed it.

A few weeks ago, Wren had accidentally built a cata-pult during a hands-on experiment. Then she'd acciden-tally shot oobleck into Axel Andrews' hair. Then she'd not so accidentally been sent to the principal's office, where she was kind of like a frequent flier.

"Hey Princess, duck!"

SMACK! A wad of paper smacked Amber's head.

"Hey!" She plucked the paper out of her long, beautiful hair and tossed it into the recycling bin.

"That Bobby!" Wren glared across the room at a boy with curly blond hair and a mischievous grin. "I swear I don't do anything worse than he does. But grownups are all 'he's just being a boy' with him and with me it's all 'go see the principal NOW young lady'! How does he always get away with it?"

Behind them, Emma stuck her tongue out at Bobby and wadded up her own paper.

"Hey, wait." Amber looked around the noisy room. "Where's Mr. Malcolm?"

"Late again." Wren pulled out her unfinished math homework and a giant eraser shaped like a cupcake. "Maybe I have a few minutes to get this torture done. I was gonna waste good eating time working on it during lunch."

And just like that, Wren was suddenly, completely absorbed in her homework.

She'd be oblivious to the world until it was done. Wren either laser-focused on one thing or was totally scattered; there was no in between. Her pencil zipped across the paper furiously while the eraser sat untouched.

Meanwhile, the rest of the class was quickly going feral. Kids launched paper wads across the room, not brave enough to leave their seats. Bobby tried to balance a wad on the back of a paper airplane. Milo, next to Bobby, wrestled to add a paper clip to the plane's nose before Bobby threw it at Emma.

"It'll go farther!" Milo laughed. "And hit harder!"

Milo didn't notice her watching him. A perfectly shaped dark ear held back a curtain of wavy black hair. From across the room Amber could see his warm brown eyes. His long eyelashes. All those beautiful white teeth.

She turned away. Milo Jones certainly hadn't noticed her dress. He never noticed her at all.

But maybe he would if she got that internship. Amber would be famous around the school. She could be the next Gail Mendez, the next Benjamin Spencer!

She knew she'd probably be competing against mostly high schoolers, but nothing ever happened if you never tried. And she had something the other kids didn't. She had the Renegade Girls Tinkering Club. They met every week in the greenhouse in Wren's backyard to make stuff, mess up, try again, eventually succeed, and just be together. The perfect group to win a contest with.

"Done!" Wren jolted Amber out of her thoughts with a final swoop of her pencil. "Victory!"

She probably got them all right too. Wren might struggle to finish her homework, but whenever she did get it done, she usually got 100%.

"How long did that take?" Wren looked around. "Jeez, Mr. Malcolm still isn't here?"

"Duck again, Princess!" Bobby hollered, standing to chuck the largest paper bomb yet.

Amber and Wren ducked.

"Do I really look like a princess?" Amber looked down at her dress. "He's the second person to say that today."

"Kinda," Wren watched Emma's return volley smack

Bobby square in the face. "With your fancy flouncy dress. Hey, where do you put your stuff? Does that thing even have pockets?"

"As a matter of fact, it does. I just wanted to look nice today."

"Sure. You know, I grew out of my last tutu in like, second grade." Wren put her homework back inside her stack of books. She usually just wore paint-stained jeans and free t-shirts from her father's video game conventions.

Amber frowned. "This is a Carpaccio, Wren, not some costume tutu. It's totally sophisticated. Not just pretty, it's designer fashion!"

"Like a grown-up princess tutu!" Wren patted the sheer overlay on Amber's skirt. "But I'm not saying you're some dumb princess, or anything."

"Why does everyone call princesses dumb anyway? In real life, they're some of the most educated people on the planet!" Amber ducked another paper bomb. "You know, Queen Elizabeth, back in the middle ages, knew like ten languages. TEN languages back when most people couldn't even read! She ruled England for almost sixty years, won lots of wars, survived assassination attempts, and made England super powerful. She fed hungry people, supported science when nobody even believed in it, and helped make the world a better place. You have to kick butt with your brain when you're a leader."

"Huh, that's cool." Wren tried to balance her cupcake eraser upside down on its frosting swirl. "You don't really think *smart* when you think *princess*."

"Yeah, exactly," Amber huffed. "And Elizabeth certainly wasn't the only princess who became a great ruler. You know what else? Queen Elizabeth never married. She didn't want anyone else in charge of her country and was afraid a husband would just take over. Back then, nobody listened to women unless they had to."

Wren snorted, "Only back then?"

"It's gotten a LITTLE better," Amber laughed. "Besides, the guy who was Elizabeth's true love wasn't royalty, so she wasn't able to marry him. Can you even imagine? Being so powerful and not being able to marry whatever person you wanted? It's so sad!"

Wren shrugged, but Amber had a dreamy look in her eyes. "And you know what else Queen Elizabeth had? An amazing wardrobe. Her clothes started trends all over the world. She had to dress really well to convince people to take her seriously. Even though she'd done all these amazing things, it was her expensive clothes that made people respect her. So she got herself the most amazing dresses in the world. Such a brilliant way to use fashion. I bet you don't think of *brilliant* and *fashion* at the same time either, huh?"

"Nope!" A paper bomb plopped on the desk in front of them. Wren tossed it to Milo, who caught it, saluted her, and spiked it on Bobby's head. "Maybe I should."

There it was. Exactly the opening Amber had been waiting for. The perfect moment to bring up the internship, even though she didn't have the flier.

"Actually," Amber began. "I wanted to talk to you. I have an idea. Something we can all do together!"

"Oooo, sounds fun." Wren leaned in conspiratorially. "What is it?"

"Well," Amber said. "I was out with my mom this weekend, and—"

CRASH!

4

SCIENCE!

*M*r. Malcolm burst through the door, breathing heavily. Everyone dropped their papers.

"BUSTED," Wren mouthed at Milo. He glared at her.

"Sorry, guys!" Mr. Malcolm headed to the front of the class. "My train was late."

"Again?" Bobby griped.

"Yup, again," Mr. Malcolm grumbled. "I hope you've all been well-behaved, despite the failings of public transportation in the most technologically advanced city in America."

He frowned at a crumpled wad of paper on his desk, tossing it into the recycling bin.

"What were you saying?" Wren whispered.

"Nothing," Amber turned to Mr. Malcolm as he began class. "I'll tell you later."

"We've been talking about the ecosystem and our place

in it." Mr. Malcolm gathered bins from the cupboard behind his desk. "Today's hands-on experiment is all about polymers. Who did the reading? Amber? What's a polymer?"

"A polymer is a big molecule made of a bunch of little repeating molecules linked together. Like a chain of paper clips," Amber obliged. "Polymers are synthetic, you know, man-made. Like plastic, polyester, or rubber."

"Right you are," he said, passing out the bins. "There are natural polymers, too, like hair or DNA."

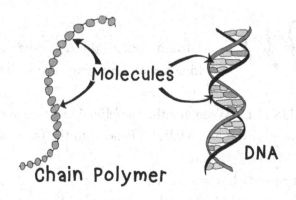

"Wait." Wren looked up at him skeptically. "You're saying people are made of plastic?"

"Nope." He paused at their table. "Plastics are just one type of polymer. Polymers are everywhere. Nice dress, Amber. You'll want to keep it covered."

Amber blushed. Mr. Malcolm moved on.

"So how are synthetic polymers made? Today, you'll be making something called bioplastic. Most plastic is made from fossil fuels like oil, which is non-renewable. Once we use up fossil fuels, they're gone. Someday we'll run out. But a bioplastic is made from something renewable, something biological."

The bin contained a carton of milk, a glass measuring cup, some food coloring, measuring spoons, craft sticks, a mug, a wire mesh strainer, a few plastic bowls, and a bunch of paper towels. Mr. Malcolm set a bottle of white vinegar on every other desk.

"The scientific method is how scientists figure stuff out. People have been refining it since the seventeenth century, so it works pretty well by now. Following the same procedure every time makes it easier to get real results, not just the results you want to see. Good science doesn't care about your feelings. It's true whether you believe it or not. The scientific method helps a scientist get to the truth and makes it easier to start answering a question."

As Mr. Malcolm handed Bobby and Milo the last bin, Amber thought about her friend Kaminia Doyle, one of the Renegades in the Tinkering Club. Kammie loved following the steps of a process. As someone smart who was easily overwhelmed, Kammie found the structure of a process helped her not panic when faced with a problem. The engineering design process had also really helped Wren channel her wild creativity. Methods and processes were really helpful!

"Today you'll be using the scientific method," Mr. Malcolm continued. "It's the process scientists use when they do research and experiments to make sure their results are real, predictable, and repeatable. That's why we believe scientists. They've been refining this process for over three hundred years, and it works pretty well by now. The scientific method gives a scientist steps to follow. Start with a question. Observe or do a little research to learn some background information. Form a hypothesis, which is an educated guess. Do an experiment to test your guess. Analyze the results of the experiment. Come to a conclusion. Finally, share that conclusion with others, who can repeat your tests."

"Yeah, we've been doing science experiments since kindergarten," Bobby impatiently shook his carton of milk.

"Sure," Mr. Malcolm nodded. "And before that even. When you were a baby, maybe you wondered, 'What would happen if I dropped this spoon?' That's asking a question. Then you guessed it might fall, based on the fact that it fell the last twenty times you dropped it, but you weren't sure. Spoons were pretty new to you back then and maybe this time would be different. So that's your hypothesis: this spoon will fall. You experimented by dropping the spoon, and observed what happened. The spoon fell. Maybe it bounced, all the food splattered everywhere, and your parents scrambled to wipe it up. So your conclusion might have been that spoons fall, food splats, and watching your parents clean up food is hilarious."

"Dad gets mad when I drop my silverware," Wren blurted.

Mr. Malcolm laughed. "Sometimes the results of an experiment will vary depending on the conditions. Like how old the spoon-dropper is. That's why scientists try to copy the exact environment and run the same experiment over and over."

"With all that in mind, our hypothesis is: we can use milk to make plastic. We're all going to run the same experiment with the same instructions, and see if we all get the same result. Let's get started."

Everyone unpacked their ingredients while Mr. Malcolm wrestled a microwave from a cupboard and plugged it in.

"Heat up the milk in here," Mr. Malcolm opened the microwave door. "You want it warm, not hot. You don't want it to burn or boil. Pour eight ounces of milk into your measuring cup — that's one cup. We can put a few in the microwave at a time and adjust the timer depending on how many cups are in there. Let's start with one minute. Meanwhile, put four teaspoons of the white vinegar in your mug."

Wren carefully poured the vinegar into a measuring spoon marked tsp, then groaned as it overflowed onto the desk.

Amber grabbed a paper towel and wiped up the spill. "Maybe you can measure it over the mug."

Wren splashed in more vinegar, this time holding the teaspoon over the mug.

"Thanks! That works better. But ewww, I hate that smell!" Wren wrinkled her nose as she handed the bottle to Emma.

"You can smell the vinegar? I didn't even notice it," Amber sniffed the air. She lifted the milk carton. "This milk is two percent. I wonder if that matters. Could you do it with skim or whole milk?"

"We could try. Is there any around?" Wren looked at the other kids' cartons as they began to mob the microwave. "It looks like everyone has the same kind. Maybe we can try different milk this weekend during the club meeting."

Amber poured the milk into the clear glass measuring cup, making sure to look at it from the side, not the top, to confirm the measurement was accurate. Once she poured the milk to the correct level, she brought it over to the microwave.

"Making a polymer is called polymerization. First you have to heat your molecule," Mr. Malcolm pushed some buttons on the microwave, which whirred and beeped. "Once the milk is warm, add it to the vinegar in the mug. Stir it gently. Milk contains proteins called casein, which link together when your warm milk meets the acidic vinegar. Watch closely and write down your observations."

Amber carefully poured the warm milk into the vinegar mug. Wren stirred it as gently as she could with a craft stick. They watched the milk spin slowly. Chunks immediately started to form.

"Look, it's getting lumpy!" Amber beamed. "I bet that's the molecules forming little chains! Look! Look! It's working!"

Wren watched the milk curdle into floating, stringy chunks. They looked kind of like jellyfish, or maybe plastic grocery bags floating in the ocean. Frowning, she wrote her observations down in the notebook she shared with Amber.

"Now, as the polymer chains coalesce, push them all together," Mr. Malcolm instructed them.

"Coh-all-ess?" Emma asked.

"Clump together," Mr. Malcolm explained. "It's a fancy way to say curdle."

Emma snorted and mumbled under her breath. "Whatever curdle means."

Amber whispered, "I think that just means when something gets lumpy."

Emma nodded and wrote something down in her notebook.

Amber glanced at Wren's notes. It did sort of look like plastic bags floating. She frowned as Wren pushed the strands together into a larger blob.

"Hey," Wren laughed. "Wouldn't it be cool if all the plastic bags in the ocean squished together to make a big plastic blob monster?"

"Plastic in the ocean isn't anything to laugh about, Wren," Amber scowled. "It's awful."

"Now you can put your strainer mesh over a bowl and strain out your polymer chains," Mr. Malcolm said. "The liquid will drain into the bowl and the chunks will stay on the mesh. Press it down to get all the water out." He handed Bobby a warm mug. "CAREFULLY."

Bobby returned to his seat and dumped all the warm milk into the mug. A lot of it sloshed onto the desk. Milo smacked him on the back of the head and picked up the stir stick. Neither of them wiped it up.

"Once you've pressed out all the liquid, dry it some

more with paper towels. Get out as much liquid as you can," Mr. Malcolm instructed. "Now, you have plastic! Just like that! Was everyone successful?"

The girls looked more closely. Their blob looked sort of like oatmeal if all the little oats were giant grains of sea salt. And it was warm.

"It looks like everyone was successful," added Mr. Malcolm, "So we can come to the conclusion that our hypothesis is correct. We CAN make plastic out of milk. This stuff will get hard once it cools and dries, but while it's warm, you can mold it and mix in some food coloring. Be careful with your food coloring; it can stain. Go ahead and play around with it, but try to keep it on your paper towels. There are lots of other types of biomass you can use to make soft plastic or clear plastic."

Wren rolled the plastic into a ball, too disgusted by the texture to ask what *biomass* meant. She tore it in two, handing one of the pieces to Amber. Then she dripped in some of their blue food coloring.

"Do people use this?" asked Wren. "To make stuff?"

"Yes," Mr. Malcolm nodded. "Scientists are using milk plastic to make more environmentally friendly food packaging, among other things. Up until about the 1950s, people used this kind of plastic all the time. They made pens, buckles, buttons, and jewelry."

"Jewelry?" Amber looked up.

"Oh yes," Mr. Malcolm smiled. "You can make really nice jewelry out of casein plastic. You can get really good quality results when you refine the process. Much better than what we're making here. They even used it for jewelry for the Queen of England."

Amber traded their blue coloring for Emma's red and began to mix. Breaking her piece up, she added different amounts of color to each piece. Maybe she could mix up some nice purples with the red and blue, and make plastic beads from three different colors.

"You can harden this plastic in the oven," Mr. Malcolm said. "But we're just going to let it dry for a few days in the windowsill. We'll observe it daily. Who thinks it will be dry tomorrow?"

Amber started to raise her hand, but saw that it was covered in red dye and little bits of plastic. Without thinking, she brushed her hands on her legs.

"Whoops!" Wren pointed at Amber's dress.

Amber looked down. An angry red smear spread viciously across the delicate lilac fabric of her dress, bold and huge. Her perfect, designer dress.

Amber screamed.

Heads snapped up as she desperately looked around for a clean paper towel. Their laughter echoed in her ears.

"Mess up your dress, Princess?" Bobby yelled. The kids laughed harder.

She wiped at the stain with her hands, forgetting they still had dye on them. The red streak got bigger. Laughter curdled in her brain until she couldn't think straight. Her expensive dress was ruined. Her beautiful outfit looked stupid. What would her mom say? What would the other kids say? This was not the way she wanted to stand out.

And the other kids wouldn't stop laughing. Somewhere in the fog of her mind, she heard Wren shouting at everyone to shut up.

"Be quiet," Mr. Malcolm snapped. "Amber, why don't you go wash that out in the bathroom?"

Amber turned and ran, tears starting to form in her eyes.

Bobby's voice trailed after her, laughing, "Waaa waaah, my dress!"

The last thing Amber saw as the door to the science room closed was Wren's cupcake eraser whizzing at Bobby's head.

BioPlastic

Materials:

Milk
Vinegar
Measuring Cup
Measuring Spoons
Wire Mesh Strainer
Paper Towels

Optional Materials:

Food Coloring
Spoon or craft stick
Bowl (or drain into sink)
Mug

Heat 8oz (1 cup) milk
(Warm, not hot)

Add 4 tsp. vinegar

Stir and observe

BAM!

You made bioplastic!

Strain through a wire mesh. Press firmly. Squeeze in paper towel.

Dry in a warm place for several days.

Add food coloring

(WARNING: Food Coloring Stains! Be super careful and don't wear a fancy dress!)

Shape with cookie cutters or poke balls with a toothpick to make beads

*A*mber punched the nozzle on the soap pump repeatedly, spurting gooey, sharp-smelling suds on her soggy skirt.

Water filled the sink and sloshed over the rim as she crammed in as much of the skirt as possible. She'd clogged the drain with paper towels so the sink would fill up. The water splashed down her legs and drenched her sequin-toed shoes, making puddles on the floor.

A lot of the stain came out with some furious scrubbing, but she kept twisting and twisting the delicate fabric angrily. Finally, she began to slow down.

Wet, blotchy wrinkles covered the damp skirt, which clung to her legs uncomfortably. Amber leaned against the sink, gazing in the mirror. Her carefully styled hair looked like she hadn't even brushed it. All that effort, and people only noticed long enough to laugh at her.

The morning had unraveled so quickly, like a torn

sweater disintegrating into a single strand of yarn. Everything had spiraled out of control with nothing she could do to stop it.

The election had been a little like that. Amber hadn't planned to run for student council. It just sort of happened. When *THE* Benjamin Spencer told her to run for a seat, how could she not? He'd looked at her with his puppy dog eyes and she'd put her name on the candidate list. The next thing she knew, life unravelled faster than she could deal with.

Of course, Benjamin was just being nice when he'd suggested it. She knew that now. He was Benjamin Spencer. All she'd done was make some spy gear. But for a moment, it had seemed like he saw something in her. Something special. And she wanted to believe he was right.

It wasn't until after the election that they'd all become friends: the Renegades, Benjamin, and Gail. At least she thought they were friends. She hadn't really talked to Benjamin or Gail since they'd caught the election thief. Maybe they were just busy getting ready for high school. Or maybe she just wasn't as special as she'd thought after all.

The door creaked open, interrupting her thoughts. A girl with a perky blond ponytail strode in. She immediately stepped in a puddle on the floor.

"Ewww! What the—" squealed Axel Andrews. Then she saw Amber at the sink. "Oh."

"Sorry!" Amber tossed the wet paper towels into the

compost bin and drained the sink. She reached over and grabbed more from the dispenser, bending down to sop up the puddles on the floor.

"Ummm, hi." Axel fidgeted awkwardly, staring down at Amber. "What are you doing?"

"Just a little accident." Amber tossed the paper towels away and stood to face Axel. They had been friends, briefly. Amber wasn't sure what they were now. "I guess it was lucky I didn't have the application with me after all!"

"Application?" Axel moved to a nearby sink and pumped some soap on her hands.

"Did you hear?" If there was anything Amber and Axel had in common, it was fashion. "Bespoke is offering a youth internship!"

"Of course! Everybody's heard about it. Didn't you read my article in the paper?" Axel wrote an events column for the school newspaper, the *Lovelace Gazette*. "Wait. You're not actually going to apply, are you?"

Amber blinked. "Well, yes. I was planning to. Aren't you?"

"Oh Amber." Axel shook her head. "Sweet Amber. You can be such a princess."

Amber didn't say anything, trying to figure out her point.

"Look, I'm trying to be nice." Axel straightened her ponytail in the mirror. "You're sweet. But let's be real. You couldn't even win the election. How can you possibly compete against high schoolers?"

"I can try." Amber crossed her arms. "You never know unless you try. So you're not applying, then?"

"Maybe I am and maybe I'm not." Axel moved toward one of the stalls. "But neither one of us stands a chance. By the way, you're going to be late for class."

Amber didn't say goodbye as she left the bathroom. Axel was probably just trying to be supportive, in her own way. But— surely she was wrong. Amber had just as good a chance as anyone. Better than most with her friends by her side. Didn't she?

The blue shoes squelched wetly on the way back to her locker. The last of the kids in the hall ran to their classes, but Amber walked slowly. The flier was still safe in the front pocket of her backpack. Someone had put her science books in her locker for her.

Wren.

Wren hadn't laughed at her. Amber had a team. With their help, she could do it, and prove Axel wrong. She'd prove them all wrong. She'd be able to talk to the Renegades about it at lunch. And lunch was only two classes away. After social studies and gym.

Gym.

She'd forgotten about gym too! Ugh! Looking down at her abused dress and sequined-toed shoes, she groaned. This was turning into a terrible day. Well, it could only get better from here.

Right?

6

ALWAYS A TEAM

*K*ids of all ages ran around the ball court and squishy-floored play structure in Lovelace's recess yard. Dark green wooden picnic tables lined the edges so the students could eat outside. The tables filled fast as kids swarmed out the door of the school in chattering groups.

The Renegades had a kind of unspoken claim to their own table. It had been their store when they sold spy gear, and now, even with their business closed, the other kids left it for them. A nice perk from when they were spies.

Amber crossed the noisy play yard toward her friends with her lunch bag in her hand. The application was nestled safely in her pocket. She'd been late to everything today, and even lunch was no exception. The other three Renegades were already eating. But at last this was it. When the day would finally turn around. The moment that would launch her career. Some day in the future, fashion magazines would write about this moment.

Amber wished she looked the part. She was a mess; dress still blotchy and wrinkled, armpits sweaty from gym class, hair stuck to her face.

And she was limping. The shoes were definitely too small. Little unwanted doubts kept creeping in, too. Axel's warning still chewed at the back of her mind. What chance did she have against high schoolers? She was just as good as any of them, she kept telling herself, especially with the help of her friends. They were a team. Once a Renegade, always a Renegade. They could do anything when they worked together. Axel just didn't understand.

"There you are." Ivy Rose Park munched on rice and strips of marinated beef from a thermos. Ivy had a reputation for being bossy, but that only was because she was great at getting stuff done. Her mom, wanting to make sure she had every advantage, had held her back a year so she'd be ready when she started kindergarten. And boy, was she ready. A whole year older than some of the kids in their grade and naturally tall to boot, Ivy had every reason to take charge. She chuckled as Amber approached. "What are you so happy about? Figured out how to make an entire backup outfit out of bioplastic?"

"Ha ha, very funny." Amber sat next to her, pulling a sandwich from her lunch bag. "Wren obviously told you about this morning."

"Seriously, though," Ivy tapped her little metal chopsticks against the side of the thermos thoughtfully.

"Clothing made of bioplastic would actually be pretty awesome. Like armor! I wonder how you could make the joints flexible."

"Are you okay?" Kaminia asked softly, gazing at her friend's clothes and hair. Kammie did everything softly. She spoke several languages, including computer programming ones, and always tried her hardest. She was one of the kindest people Amber knew. But since she hardly ever spoke to anyone except her friends, only the Renegades knew the secret of how amazing she was.

"Yes, thanks." Amber took a deep breath, "but I do have something to tell you guys. I was at Bespoke last weekend and have amazing news!"

"Bespoke?" Wren choked through a mouthful of bagel. "Your favorite fancy-pants fashion-clothes place? What did you buy now?"

"Nothing." Amber glanced down at the application under the table. "I didn't see anything good. Anyway—"

"Nothing good?" Kammie giggled. "Don't tell us you've grown tired of that place!"

"Seriously, Kammie? No, I just didn't have much time." Amber held the application out to them triumphantly. She tried not to squeal with excitement. "Bespoke is having a contest for a YOUTH INTERNSHIP position! You guys, we could totally do it!"

She looked around excitedly, waiting. But no one said anything. They just stared at her, confused. The silence dragged on and Amber's beaming smile faded. Ivy coughed and looked away.

Amber tried again. "I hoped we could turn in the application this weekend. Together, as a team. Instead of meeting at the Greenhouse because —"

"Go to Bespoke?" Wren interrupted. She'd tried to go to Bespoke with Amber once before. The trip had been a disaster. She'd had no reason to go back since. "Really? I don't have the money to spend in a place like that."

"That's not —" Amber started.

"Look, Amber, I know you really like it there." Ivy twisted the lid back on her thermos. "But our club time is supposed to be for serious science work. Not fashion time."

"Hey, that's not fair," Amber stammered. "Science is my life, you know that. I don't see any of you memorizing genus and species names for fun. Like that *sciurus griseus* over there."

A gray squirrel (or, to Amber, a *sciurus griseus*) scampered across the fence that surrounded the play yard, someone's bag of Cheetos clamped firmly in its little mouth. Chunks of bright orange dropped along its path as the squirrel leapt across the fence. A group of young boys bolted after it, screaming. One of them picked up the escaped Cheetos from the ground and stuffed them into his mouth.

Wren gagged.

"Yeah, I get it, you know science stuff," Ivy continued. "But look, things are getting complicated now that we're in middle school. Assignments are harder, and I have to really dedicate myself if I want to stay in both soccer AND basketball. I hardly have time for the club at all. I want to spend it making stuff. What's the point of using valuable club time on clothes? I hate shopping, it's a waste of time."

"It's not about shopping, it's an internship! And just because you don't like shopping doesn't mean no one else does," Amber said, feeling the blood rising in her face. She wasn't sure if she was embarrassed or mad, but she felt backed into a corner.

"Jeez, don't be mad, Amber. Sorry, but you totally took that the wrong way." After a tense second, Ivy took a deep breath and glanced at the flier. "Look, we've been trying to figure out ways to repair the microscope. That takes money. Internships aren't like jobs. You probably wouldn't get paid. The whole internship would probably be taking out the trash and cleaning the changing rooms or something. And for what? To figure out what's in style this week? We need to spend our time making money for the club or doing club stuff. There's nothing tinkery about fashion."

Amber pursed her lips. Were they right? Suddenly she wasn't so sure. Was sewing not the same as inventing? Was finding the right type of fabric really that different than finding the right kind of cardboard? It felt the same to her. She didn't really see the difference between making an outfit and building spy gear. Was she wrong? What made any type of inventing and creating less valid than any other type?

Axel's words came back to her. Was she being naive? Maybe applying for the internship was a stupid idea after all. It was too big. Too ambitious. She certainly couldn't compete without her friends.

But this opportunity might never come again. Shouldn't she at least try? Amber's head spun. She had no idea what to do. There had to be something that would convince them that fashion wasn't worthless. An idea flashed in her mind. She suddenly remembered a sign in the window in the store her mom had parked in front of, two doors down from Bespoke.

"Okay, well, how about this? There's a new place, a consignment store called Bygone. Obviously copying Bespoke. So rude! Anyway, they buy clothes," Amber explained. If there was anything Amber had, it was clothes.

"Yeah. That's what a consignment store does." Wren crammed a handful of potato chips into her mouth and talked around them. "Buys good quality used clothes and sells them cheap."

Amber nodded. "They're specifically looking for tween and young teen sizes. We could sell some clothes on Saturday to get money for the new eyepieces. They're buying until four o'clock."

"Really? That's kinda cool." Wren wiped the crumbs off her mouth and dumped the rest of the chips on the picnic table in front of her, arranging them in order from smallest to largest. "I've never seen a consignment store in San Francisco that carries tween sizes. The ones in the Haight are for grown-ups and the ones in Noe Valley and Bernal are for babies. Maybe it's worth a visit. I'm running out of pants."

"Huh, that's not a bad idea," Ivy nodded thoughtfully. "I wonder how much money we can make there."

"I'll ask my Mom if she can take us." Amber watched Wren smash the leftover potato chips one by one.

"Oh! Great timing," Kammie nodded. "I'm supposed to clean my room for Diwali. It's all about renewal. Cleaning and purging old stuff is part of the celebration. Mom would be thrilled if I got rid of some clothes."

"A holiday about cleaning?" Wren laughed. "What kind of wacky tradition is that?"

"No, it's super fun!," Kammie smiled. "The purging is just part of it. The festival of lights is five days long. It's a big party. But Mom uses it as an excuse to make me clean out my room and get rid of old stuff. Which is dumb because we never host so its not like anybody is going to be checking my closet. And honestly, nobody really cares. Or, at least nobody we celebrate with anyway. People are too busy hanging out and having fun. Everybody gets dressed up and the food is amazing. We even went to celebrate with the family in India once."

"Do you wear a sari?" Amber tried to picture Kammie dressed up in the traditional Indian clothes she'd seen in movies: a brightly colored long silk skirt and half shirt with an even more gorgeous silk scarf draped over one shoulder, extending to the floor in the front and back. "Those are so lovely!"

"A sari?" Kammie laughed. "No, I'm not old enough. Mom says not until I turn sixteen. I just wore a regular salwar kameez. A tunic and leggings. But it was really pretty."

"Oh," Amber blushed. "I didn't know you had to be a certain age to wear a sari."

Kammie shrugged. "It's sort of like wearing makeup. Everybody has their own rules. My mom is pretty strict about it."

"Oh hey," Wren interrupted. "The art store is right near Bespoke. Mom and Trixie are going on Saturday to get some stuff for Mom's new yarn arts class. We can be another car."

"Yeah, okay. Let's do it," Ivy agreed. "Let's make some money."

Well, at least she was contributing, Amber thought. She might not become a famous designer by selling clothes, but just maybe she could be a hero and earn enough money to fix their broken microscope.

Heading back into school, Amber pulled the flier out of her pocket. Secretly, she glanced at it one more time, running her thumb longingly over the words at the bottom. They said: DEADLINE TO APPLY - November 10th.

Saturday would be the 10th.

7

BYGONE

"Somebody forgot to color the sky." Wren climbed out of her mom's Prius, shifting her backpack, and turned to wave through the car window at her mom.

The Prius pulled out of the loading zone into traffic in search of a real parking spot. Horns blared and fast-moving cars swerved to avoid it. Mrs. Rosenberg's Tesla pulled into the loading zone and the other girls stepped out.

The San Francisco fog chilled them as soon as they were on the sidewalk. Kammie, Amber, and Ivy snuggled into their fleeces as Wren zipped up her too-large hoodie with a game company logo on the back. More free video game swag inherited from her dad.

Across the windows of the store behind them, in gold Victorian-style letters, the words *BYGONE* glowed brightly in the gray morning like a beacon.

"It's ON!" Amber plopped a laundry bag full of clothes on the sidewalk. "I'm ready to make some money."

"You're really bringing your A game!" Ivy gasped as Amber grabbed a second giant bag from her mom's Tesla.

"I'm in it to win it, Ivy," Amber replied, her head inside the car. "These clothes might just earn enough money to get a whole new microscope, not just the eyepieces!"

It might not have been her original plan, but now that they were here, Amber was pretty excited. The internship application was tucked into her pocket, just in case. There might still be a chance to apply, if they changed their minds at the last minute.

"This is a white zone, sweetie. I can't stay here." Amber's mom shoved her third bag out the door. It smacked flat on the sidewalk in front of them. "You were supposed to catch that. I'll find parking and see you all inside."

Her car zipped away too, leaving the girls alone on the sidewalk surrounded by bags.

"Wow, this store does look a lot like that fancy-pants Bespoke place," Wren said. "You weren't kidding that they're trying to copy." Wren pointed two doors down to another store with swirly letters crawling all over its windows.

The boutique's massive door opened. A girl with a perky blond ponytail stepped out and moved down the sidewalk in the opposite direction. Axel? And next to her... Amber's heart skipped a beat. A boy with dark wavy hair.

A boy casually slouching down the sidewalk in a very familiar way.

Milo?

What was Milo doing at Bespoke? With Axel? Amber turned away, catching her breath. When she looked again, the pair were halfway down the block, too far away for Amber to be sure. Maybe it wasn't them at all. San Francisco was a big place. They could be anybody. And anyway, it wasn't any of her business.

Suddenly deflated, Amber hefted one of her bags awkwardly onto her shoulder. It covered most of her face. Hugging a second bag around the middle with her other arm, she tried to kick the third into the store.

"I got it." Wren just had a backpack. She grabbed the bag away from Amber's foot.

Kammie carried a few paper grocery bags of neatly folded clothes. Ivy gripped a half-empty plastic garbage bag.

Amber reached for Bygone's door handle. The bag on her shoulder shifted, and the door slammed shut while she wrestled it back into place. A voice came from the other side of the bag against her face, the speaker blocked mostly from view.

"Whoa, let me get that for you, Princess," it said. "Are you going to try to sell all those? Yikes!"

Blue-tipped, spiky hair was all she could see of the person holding the door.

"Yeah, thanks," she told the hair while maneuvering through the door.

Bygone looked a lot like Bespoke on the inside, too. Tall glass cases filled with jewelry surrounded the register by the front doors. Racks of used clothes and shoes filled the interior. The changing rooms and a small seating area were in the back.

Amber looked around uncertainly. Wren, however, pushed past dragging Amber's bag towards a little counter in the back. A line of other people holding bags snaked along the wall.

Wren joined the back of the line. "Come on, guys."

Amber and the others joined her tentatively.

"What's this line for?" Amber asked.

"It's the selling line," Wren laughed. "Haven't you ever sold clothes at a consignment store before?"

Amber plopped down her bags. Honestly, she hadn't ever even been inside a consignment store before. Judging from the clothes along the wall, though, this buyer had great taste. She ran her hand over a soft, fluffy cotton sweater on a nearby rack and checked the price out of curiosity. It cost a fraction of what she'd expect for such a nice sweater. This wasn't from any inexpensive mall store; this sweater was high-end.

"Wow," she mumbled. "What a great deal!"

"Oh jeez." Wren rolled her eyes. "Can't you stop shopping for a minute?"

Amber quickly put the sweater back. "I was just looking."

"I'm not sure you'll survive this trip without a few new clothes!" Ivy teased.

45

"I'll try to control myself," Amber groaned. "We need money for the microscope."

Suddenly, out of nowhere, a small human-shaped missile hurdled towards her screaming, "AMBER!"

Amber and the child projectile crashed into the clothes behind them as Amber's bags flopped over. The sticky face of Wren's little sister, Trixie, smiled up adoringly at Amber.

"Mama got me a bunch of yarn for my birthday!" Trixie had just turned six about a week ago. "I got whatever I wanted from the sale basket! Wanna see?"

She shoved a bulging shopping bag in Amber's face. Off in the racks, Amber saw her mom talking with Wren's mom. They looked content to browse while the girls went through the buyer's line.

Amber pushed the bag of yarn down, looking around the store. People of all ages pulled hangers off racks and pressed dresses against each other happily. In front of them in line stood a few guys and two women. As she watched, one walked away from the buyer's counter, pocketing some cash.

The buyer turned out to be the person attached to the door-opening blue hair. She looked kind of young, but Amber assumed she must be an adult. Her hazel eyes were huge and round in a heart-shaped face. She had a strong nose and pointy chin. Even though she looked small and unassuming behind the counter, she clearly knew what she was doing. She moved through each seller's clothes confidently, briefly chatting with them. More than a handful of clothes earned a seller a numbered card. The blue-haired buyer then clipped an identical card to their bag and called up the next seller. No wonder the line was moving so quickly.

The buyer perked up as Wren tossed her backpack onto the counter. "Fabulous! Did you bring in some teen clothes?" She beamed at the four of them like it was Christmas. "I really need to flesh out the Juniors section!"

Amber felt a surge of pride, but sighed as Wren pulled just two pairs of jeans, a sweater, and a dress out of her backpack. *Oh Wren,* Amber chuckled in her head. *That's okay, I have plenty of clothes to make up for it.*

The buyer got to business, carefully inspecting each piece and checking the brand and content labels. Was she older than Amber thought? Hard to tell. She set one pair of Wren's jeans aside. Running a finger along the seams of the remaining three items, she paid especially close attention to the dress.

"Nice stuff," she complimented Wren. "I take it it's not your first time in a consignment shop. I like these three. This dress is a real Carpaccio! Fabulous!"

"Thanks!" Wren beamed as the buyer pulled a stack of bills from under her counter. "I got it from my cousin. I even wore it to a party once."

She happily accepted the bills and stuffed the rejected jeans into her backpack. The buyer dumped the items into a giant rolling laundry bin, and motioned Ivy over.

She only took two of Ivy's pieces from the dozen in the bag. Amber wasn't surprised. They were mainly boring, practical clothes. In exchange for her two bags, Kammie got a little plastic card.

Then, finally, it was Amber's turn.

"Okay, Princess," Blue-hair smirked at the three enormous bags. "What have you got for me?"

Amber maneuvered her bags onto the counter. The buyer began to paw through them.

"We're raising money for our club," Amber babbled, suddenly a little self-conscious.

"What club is that?" Blue-hair said offhandedly, not really paying attention. "Spa club or babysitting? You guys make YouTube channels about your favorite celebrity crushes?"

Anger poked at the corners of Amber's nervousness. "Actually, we're a science and tinkering club. We do scientific research and invent and build things from scratch."

Blue-hair looked up at her. Amber looked back.

"Interesting," Blue-hair drawled. "What kind of science?"

It felt like a test. Amber was good at tests.

"My specialty is biology and natural science. I want to be a biologist when I grow up." It didn't feel like a complete enough answer, so she added, "At the moment I'm researching native San Francisco trees, unlike the *Acacia baileyana* out front. It's a lovely tree but technically an invasive species from Australia."

"BAM!" Wren's voice boomed from the seating area nearby, "You just got SCIENCED!"

Blue-hair broke out laughing. "Awesome! I sure did! I love it! You had me fooled with your princess act."

Amber faltered. "What act? I love fashion."

"So, what are you?" The woman smirked. "A princess or a scientist?"

"Why does everyone keep asking me that?" Amber threw up her hands. "Why do I have to be one or the other?"

The woman looked at her more closely with a thoughtful expression. Just then, Trixie popped her head over the counter.

"Hi lady, my name's Trixie," she blurted. "What's your name?"

"Hello Trixie, what a great name," Blue-hair smiled down at her.

"It's actually Beatrix. But my sister didn't like that as much, so she changed it."

"Well," Blue-hair confided. "I'm just Juliana. That's not as fun as your name, but you can call me Jules."

"Jewels?" Trixie stared at Juliana. "That's so pretty! I like sparkles! Your hair is pretty. Amber has a jewel name, too."

Juliana stared at her in confusion for a second. Then she laughed.

"No, not jewel like jewelry, like diamonds, just Jules. J-U-L-E-S." She paused and added, "But, you know what? You can spell it any way you want, Trixie. I think I like your way better. And how about you?"

Amber held out her hand, "I'm Amber. Rosenberg."

Jewels, shaking her hand, glanced at the line behind Amber. "It's been nice chatting with you, Science Princess Amber Rosenberg. I have to keep the line moving, but you've given me some stuff to think about. Here's your ticket. I'll call you when I've sorted your stuff."

Amber accepted the ticket and moved into the seating area nearby to wait with her friends.

8

SELLING FASHION

*J*ewels shut down the line two customers after them and now busily sorted, stacked, and calculated the bags she'd set aside, including Amber's and Kammie's. The girls had grabbed all the seats by the nearby changing rooms, so the other sellers had to wander the store while waiting to be called back.

From her seat, Amber watched Jewels dump the laundry bags out on the sorting counter. A warm feeling grew inside her with every piece Jewels tossed into a growing mound.

"What is it you like so much about fashion, anyway?" Wren watched Amber watch Jewels. Trixie squeezed into the seat next to her and stuck her face into the yarn bag.

Amber didn't answer immediately. How could she explain? Combining colors, patterns, shapes, materials... it wasn't just fun, it felt really good. When she looked confident, she felt confident. She liked crafting together a beautiful outfit. It felt like art. And like it or not, everyone judged people on what they looked like. Queen Elizabeth had been right. The right clothes made you feel regal. And when you felt it, other people did too.

Why did so many people think that if you liked fashion, you couldn't like anything else? Nobody thought her father couldn't like football and still have an important job. And he REALLY liked football. But people sometimes thought her mother didn't have any job at all if she shopped for a lot of clothes. They said her husband must have given her a credit card, even though she knew her mom actually made more money than her dad. It didn't make sense.

"It's hard to explain," she replied finally.

"I like clothes that let me move," Ivy offered. "Stretchy fabrics that wick up my sweat so I don't get all gross."

"Wick?" asked Trixie. "Like a candle?"

"Wicking means sucking. Like sucking a drink through a straw."

"Your clothes drink your sweat?" Trixie gagged. "GROSS!!"

Jewels looked over at them. She turned back to her sorting, but shifted closer and kept an ear pointed at them.

Ivy smiled. "More like when a towel dries you off after a bath. It sucks away the wet stuff. Anyway, any pair of pants that bends with my legs and doesn't pull down off my butt is fashionable enough for me!"

"It takes a lot of science to make fabric like that,"

Amber pointed out. "Wren, do you remember that report I did for Mr. Malcolm's class about a famous scientist?"

"Which one?" Wren asked. "Wait, are you talking about the bullet lady?"

"Bullet PROOF," Amber corrected. "Stephanie Kwolek, the chemist who invented bulletproof fabric. Well, bullet-resistant is the proper term. It's called Kevlar. It's like armor but flexible and easy to wear. They make bullet-proof vests out of it. It's even used in space suits. I mean, imagine the amount of science in a space suit! It has to keep astronauts from freezing and not let oxygen leak out, but it still has to be flexible. I can't even imagine how much science goes into that! But even the fabric they make normal clothes out of is amazing."

"What's amazing about it?" asked Ivy skeptically.

"For starters," Amber said, "there are the fibers themselves, both natural and synthetic. Like polyester, for example. You know how we were talking about polymers in science? The long chains of molecules? That's where *polyester* gets its name. It's a polymer made from something called ester. It's synthetic — you know, man-made, like plastic. Not natural like cotton. They made polyester because they wanted stronger, less wrinkly fabric. Ivy's athletic clothes have so much science in them. To stretch, wick sweat, not wrinkle, and move with your body. Do you know how much research goes into that?"

"Really?" Kammie asked. "That's cool."

"Huh," Ivy mused. "How DOES fabric stretch? I guess I always thought...I don't know, that it just did."

"Natural fibers don't stretch much. So scientists made synthetic ones," Amber replied. "They used chemistry and science to make elastic fabric. Stretchy fabric. Before that, the only way to get fabric to stretch was by weaving it a certain way."

Ivy stretched the material on her shirt, watching it expand and contract.

"How do you make a non-stretchy fiber stretch?" asked Kammie.

"That sounds like an engineering problem, not a fashion problem," Wren said. "Or, well, maybe both. It's engineering solving a fashion problem."

"You wouldn't believe how much engineering, science, and math go into fashion," Amber explained. "So there are two main types of fabric: knit and woven. Knit fabric is made out of yarn looping into itself, so it can move and pull in different directions. That's how it stretches even though the fibers don't. Like the links of a chain! The chain can bend around but none of the links bend."

"Like KNIT knit?" Wren moved her hands around probably imitating knitting needles, but it actually just looked like she was swatting away a swarm of flies. "I thought that was just a silly thing that grandmas do. Well, grandmas and my weird mom."

"Yeah," Amber nodded. "Lots of stuff grandmas do is full of science and math. Knitting, quilting, cross-stitch, macrame, stuff like that. People just don't give it the credit it deserves. Granny's tried to teach me a lot of it, but I like sewing best. Macrame makes my head hurt. But anyway, back to knits. T-shirt fabric is knitted kind of like a sweater, but with thread instead of yarn. The thread is so small you can't even see the knit."

"You could if you used a microscope, I bet!" Wren added enthusiastically. She elbowed Ivy, who seemed to be deep in thought. "I want to go back and look at my shirt now!"

"You know so much about fabric, Amber." Kammie held the sleeve of her shirt up close to her face, trying to see the weave.

"You have to when you make your own clothes. How heavy a fabric is, how it hangs, what it's made of, and whether it stretches or not all affect how your clothes turn out."

Ivy didn't say anything. She still looked lost in thought.

"What about not stretchy fabric? Is that knitted too?" Wren waved her hands around wildly again, apparently still pretending to knit.

"No." Amber sat up straighter. "Woven fabric is like a fancier version of those loom art projects we used to do in school."

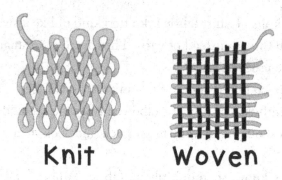

Knit   Woven

"Like weaving potholders on those red plastic looms? That's kid stuff," Ivy frowned.

"I loved doing the loom!" Wren said. "But I completely forgot how to do it."

"We did weaving in art class last week," Trixie pouted. "But mine got messed up. I went under and under instead of over and under."

"Yeah, like that. Here, I can show you." Amber looked around, making a scissor motion with her fingers. "Anybody have some scissors?"

To her surprise, Jewels, without looking up from her sorting, handed over a pair.

"Trixie, can I borrow some of your yarn?"

Trixie handed over a ball of brown yarn with a pout. Amber pulled a long length from it, snipped it off and handed it back to Trixie. Then she grabbed a white ball as well, pulling and snipping a piece of that, too. Trixie grabbed it back and clutched the bag possessively.

"If I had some cardboard, or one of those red plastic

looms, this would be easier to show," Amber mumbled. "But for now, I'll do it Renegade style!"

Amber grabbed Wren's arm, placing her hand in the middle of the group so they could all see it. Wren's palm pointed down.

"Okay." Amber loosely wrapped the brown thread around Wren's hand several times. She took the white thread and threaded it over, under, over, and under the brown strands. Then she went back through, lacing it the opposite way, going over on a strand she'd gone under, and under on a strand she'd gone over. She laced a few more rows until she had a simple weave. "So a plain, basic weave is just like all those art projects in school. That's how they make woven fabric."

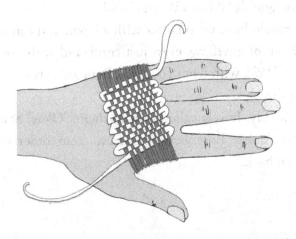

She handed the scissors back to Jewels, who took them without looking up. Amber looked at her curiously for a second. How did she know? Then she shrugged and turned back to her example.

"But see, you can make cool patterns by mixing up how you weave it. Or even how fat or thin the yarns are. Sometimes they mix a fat string and a thin string. Sometimes they weave in a pattern and do under, under, over, under, under, over or whatever. It makes the fabric look, feel, and move differently. Plaids are made by weaving different colors in the same order over and over again."

"That makes sense," Kammie nodded. "Anything you do over and over again is a pattern. One little change, over time, makes a whole different pattern. I do that in coding but haven't ever thought about it for fabric."

Amber finished weaving a little square of cloth from the yarn, and slid it from Wren's hand.

"It would have been better with a loom. You can make a loom out of anything, even just cardboard with notches cut in it. Work with what you have, Renegade style, right?" Amber shrugged.

Suddenly, Jewels called over to them. "Okay, Science Princess Amber Rosenberg and crew. Your order is up. Come on back."

Fancy

Materials:
- Yarn, ribbon, string, strips of paper, or even rubber bands
- Scissors
- Corrugated Cardboard

Optional:
- Thumbtacks

MAKE YOUR OWN LOOM

Cut an equal number of slots in the top & bottom of a cardboard rectangle.

Glue two cardboard rectangles together to make them thicker, and stick an equal number of thumbtacks

-OR-

in the top & bottom.

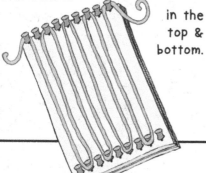

Patterns

- "1up" means weave over
- "1down" means weave under
- "..." means "repeat"
- Each row is a line

so this pattern is: 1up, 1down...
1down, 1up...

Weaves

WEAVE PATTERNS - Plan with a grid

One color for
one yarn

Another color
for the other

1up, 1down...
1down, 1up...

2up, 2down...
2down, 2up...

3up, 1down...
3down, 1up...

Get Fancy!

2up, 1down...
3up, 3down...
2down, 1up...
3down, 3up...
5down, 1up...

Go Diagonal!

First Diagonal
2up, 1down...

Other Diagonal,
(third color)
2down, 1up...

Also
try:

Circle Loom
Fat&Thin Yarns
What else?

9

VERDICT

"You know she's right." Jewels leaned on her elbows. "The fashion industry is full of top-notch science and technology — always has been. The invention of fabric was a pretty big moment in human development."

"But that's not actually fashion," Ivy scoffed.

"Isn't it, Sporty?" Jewels raised her eyebrows. "Isn't it? Now, you, I'm sorry I didn't get your name?"

She looked at Kammie expectantly. Kammie froze like a deer in headlights.

Wren answered for her. "That's Kammie. Kaminia."

Jewels looked from Wren to Kammie, then shrugged. "Okay Kammie Kaminia, I took this pile here. And here are the ones I couldn't take." She slid about half of the clothes back into one of the bags and offered her a few bills.

Two piles remained on the counter. Amber saw with pride that one of the piles was huge, and the other just had a few small pieces in it. How much money was she going to get for all that? For sure enough to fix the microscope. Maybe they'd be looking at different fabric weaves together by the end of the day!

Jewels pulled out Amber's laundry bags. Amber stepped forward with her head held high.

Then, instead of sweeping the few pieces in the small pile into a laundry bag to return, Jewels tipped the giant pile into bag after bag, handing each to an incredulous Amber.

"But," Amber stammered. "But...you aren't taking these? But...why not?"

Jewels looked at her sympathetically.

"Oh Science Princess Amber Rosenberg, I'm so sorry, honestly. Most of your clothes are fast fashion. The kind of clothes you see at the mall, the kind that are made fast and worn fast and gotten rid of fast. The kind that change style all the time, to make you keep buying new clothes. They're too trendy for me. If they don't sell in a month, they'll already be out of style, and I'll be stuck with them forever. Besides, even if I could sell them, I wouldn't make very much money on them. I only have so much space in the store, I need to fill it with high-quality stuff that won't go out of style next week."

Jewels pointed to the racks in the store. Amber remembered the sweater she'd seen earlier. It wasn't something she'd get in a mall store, that was true. And the quality had been spectacular at a really low price. How cheap would

Jewels have to sell clothes used if someone could get them for a few bucks brand new?

"Plus, the quality of fast fashion is really bad. I mean, those cheap mall store fashions LOOK nice for a little while, but they're cheap for a reason. Look." Jewels took one of the shirts and ran her finger along a seam. The finger popped right through halfway down. "The quality just isn't there. If it isn't the seams, the super thin fabric gets little holes in it, like rodents chewed it. These clothes are only meant to last a few months. They want you to keep buying new ones, keep spending money at the store. I just can't take this stuff."

Amber couldn't speak. She wasn't going to save the day. She wasn't going to fix the microscope. Her fashion was worthless. "But...what am I supposed to do with all these clothes?"

"Yeah," Jewels nodded sadly. "That's the question, isn't it? What happens to it? Don't throw it in the trash...the landfills are packed full of millions of tons of old clothes. Actually, some of the mall stores pretend to be eco-conscious by accepting the old stuff for recycling, and San Francisco has a fabric recycling program, but honestly I don't know how much of this stuff actually gets recycled in the end. You could try Goodwill. But again, whatever they don't sell usually goes straight to the landfill."

Jewels slid a few dollars over apologetically and said something Amber didn't hear as she tried to process what was happening.

"I..." Amber looked up at the Renegades. "I don't think this is even close to enough."

Everyone else pressed their money into Kammie's hands for her to count. Wren turned her back towards Jewels for the first time.

Jewels gasped.

"Whoa! You...you there...Science Princess Amber Rosenberg's friend!" Jewels reached over the counter for Wren's sleeve. "Wait! Is that a real development team jacket from the original 4Bloks team?"

Wren looked down at her hoodie. It had a company logo with a year under it on the back. She shrugged. "Yeah, I guess so. My dad is always bringing home hoodies from the games he works on. He's the lead programmer on 4Bloks Ultra now."

"I mean. Wow." Jewels sat back, her eyes wide, and rubbed her spiky blue hair.

The other Renegades knew the video game Wren and Trixie's dad worked on was super popular. Everybody knew 4Bloks. But it was a grown-up's game. They didn't play it, so they usually forgot about it.

"That jacket!" Jewels waved her hands at the hoodie. "It's from the very first release!"

"Yeah?" Wren shrugged again. "Dad was one of the original devs, the people who made the game. He was, like, NEVER home when Trixie was born. It really sucked. Sometimes he'd sleep there. That was before his company got bought and stuff."

"I don't suppose you want to sell it, do you?" Jewels

pleaded. "It's a lot to ask, I know, but most of my customers here are young techie guys and they would KILL for that hoodie. It's not a size extra-large by any chance, is it?"

Wren shook her head, taking the hoodie off. "Just a large. You still want it? I have a bunch more back home. Two more from this same year, in fact."

Jewels took the hoodie excitedly and handed Wren as much money as the four of them had made that day combined.

Amber should have been ecstatic. But instead, she was jealous. SHE was the fashion girl. Wren hadn't even done anything on purpose. She didn't know anything about fashion! Amber yanked her rejected laundry bags irritably out of the way as Jewels carefully folded Wren's stupid hoodie.

"I still don't think this is enough money for the eyepieces, but we're a lot closer!" Kammie counted the bills several times to be sure.

Ivy turned to Amber. "I owe you an apology. There really is more to clothes than Paris Fashion Week."

"What's Paris Fashion Week?" Wren asked.

Amber ignored them both.

"I sure didn't know fabric was that interesting." Kammie shoved the money in her pocket and looked excitedly from Wren to Ivy. "Did you?"

"No. I had no idea," Ivy admitted, "I didn't think there was anything interesting about fashion at all. Mom always said there's no point in all that girly stuff. We don't do makeup or anything. It's not practical. But, I don't know, the science behind fashion is actually kinda interesting. So,

I guess I'm trying to say I'm sorry if you were hurt by what I said at lunch."

"So what I love isn't completely worthless? Gee, thanks, Ivy." Amber narrowed her eyes angrily. She didn't even know why she was so angry, but it bubbled up inside her like lava. "But honestly? That's a really dumb apology."

Ivy blinked. "What do you mean? I'm trying to say I'm sorry and I was wrong."

"No, you're not." Amber pursed her mouth. "If you want to say you're sorry and you're wrong, just say it. You're saying the stuff I love isn't worth anything unless you like it too. I don't like running around and getting sweaty, but that doesn't mean basketball is pointless, you know? You aren't apologizing for judging me, you're apologizing for, I don't even know. For the fact that I got hurt by you hating on stuff I like? Why do people hate girly stuff so much? What's the difference between liking a basketball and liking a unicorn?"

"Well, to start with," Ivy began, putting her hands on her hips, "a basketball is real. It's important. A unicorn is fantasy."

"No it's not!" shouted Trixie.

Jewels looked over at them as she handed some clothes back to another seller.

"It doesn't matter, Trixie, Ivy doesn't get it." Amber knew she was taking her frustration out on Ivy but couldn't stop herself. "It's not hard to respect things other people like. I don't like basketball. I think it's stupid to go around and memorize stats and plays and jersey numbers. But I don't make fun of you when you do it. And I don't think it makes you a dumb jock."

"What do you want from me? I'm sorry. Look, sometimes it's hard to apologize." Ivy threw up her hands in frustration. "At least I'm trying."

Amber wasn't sure it was ever hard to apologize. Sometimes she apologized too much.

"Well, I'm glad you had the idea to come here today," Kammie said softly. "We earned some money, learned interesting stuff, and found a new store. I'm sorry we teased you. And I'd love to know more about weaving and fabric and everything. I think you should apply for that internship. I'd be up for helping."

"Me too," Wren agreed.

Ivy still looked doubtful, but nodded hesitantly.

"Really?" Amber breathed hopefully. "I mean, apparently my taste in fashion stinks. Do you think we have a chance?"

"You know what, Science Princess Amber Rosenberg?" Jewels surprised them. They hadn't known she was listening. "I think you should go for it. The fashion world needs more people like you."

Amber hesitated. She was suddenly nervous. She wanted this internship so much, but now, after her failure at selling her clothes, she wasn't sure she could compete.

"Come on!" Wren pushed Amber out the door.

rystal chandeliers hung from the ceiling of Bespoke, glittering with gentle miniature rainbows. The sun had finally, briefly, eaten away the grayness, and light streamed through the front windows onto dazzling racks of fine fabrics. Moments later, the clouds swallowed everything again. A mannequin posed on top of every rack, hips thrust to the side, arms splayed out, draped in velvets, satins, and stylishly subdued linens. Wren carefully avoided the racks, as if she might accidentally nudge one and be crushed by a toppling, fabulously stylish statue. She fidgeted uncomfortably, but Amber felt like she was coming home.

Amber flashed back to being eight years old. Tiny, and desperate to look like a big kid, too small to fit in the clothes she wanted to wear, not happy with the clothes she did fit in. So Granny taught her to sew. She remembered clearly the day they walked into the fabric store, the moment that had changed her life. The moment she realized she had power. If the world didn't make clothes she felt proud to wear, she could make them herself. She could make anything, literally make her dreams come true with enough time, knowledge, and maybe a little help.

Back then, Granny had shown her how to cut, pin, and sew, and Amber never stopped sewing. Even when she started shopping in the big kids' section. Even as her wardrobe expanded to include more and more store-bought clothes, she still sewed. At eleven, Amber knew the ins and outs of buttonholing, interfacing, and the correct way to place pins so she could pull them out before the sewing machine needle snapped on them. She needed her grandma's help for complicated things like zippers, but by now she could do a lot by herself.

Bespoke designed and created its own high-end outfits. Everything was one-of-a-kind. And to Amber's constant amazement, it carried clothes for everyone, even kids. Juniors' sizes and little kid sizes. There were clothes for men and women of all shapes and sizes. The glass cabinets near the register housed all sorts of accessories, too.

It was almost like the owner designed whatever they felt like, then made it without caring too much about who was going to buy it. Amber had never met the owner, so she had no idea who they were, what they looked like, or what they'd been thinking, but judging from their work-manship, they truly cared about what they were doing. And maybe they were a little crazy, too.

A tiny sliver of hope broke through Amber's sadness. If she really could get an internship here, well, it would be something truly special. She'd be part of something meaningful. But did she even stand a chance? She looked around and suddenly realized how crowded the store was.

"There weren't nearly this many people here last weekend," Amber whispered to Wren nervously.

The place was packed. Behind Amber and Wren, Ivy strode confidently past the crowd and immediately started looking for the box to deposit Amber's application.

Kammie, however, froze in the doorway. A lanky boy, about fifteen years old, with warm brown skin and scruffy bleached hair, pushed past her. Kammie scampered into the corner by the door. The boy wore eyeliner, tight black jeans with a loose creamy t-shirt, a soft gray scarf, and a deep teal cardigan. He carried a flier just like Amber's.

Wren tugged on Amber's sleeve and pointed out the flier. They stood together, rooted in place, watching the boy bring it confidently to the counter and try to drop it in an overflowing box. The paper didn't fit so he shoved it in with one blue-fingernailed hand.

Suddenly, Amber noticed teenagers everywhere. A girl with impeccable highlights in her long, glamorous hair wore a flowing dress of pink and orange gauze, dip-dyed like the sunset. She chatted casually with another girl with short, sleek hair that was so black it shone blue. She wore fishnet stockings, black motorcycle boots, and a leather jacket over purple cut-off chain-laden jean shorts and a plain white t-shirt. They both looked like they were in high school. A bored-looking girl chewed gum loudly and leaned against the counter. Her gorgeous black hair, in a billion little braids, swung over her dark skin and tight black turtleneck. A diamond necklace hung all the way to the waist of her trim white jeans. Her tan cardigan slouched stylishly off one shoulder. Her thigh-high boots had heels so high, Amber didn't understand why she didn't fall on her face. The girl pulled a flier out of her Gucci purse and absently stuffed it into the overflowing box before somehow looking elegant as she turned and clicked her heels out the door. Trixie, entering the store with both moms, pointed at the girl excitedly as she passed. The older girl nodded at Trixie, not even stumbling in those shoes.

Something inside Amber broke. Axel was right. What was she even doing here? Who did she think she was? She turned terrified eyes to Wren.

Ivy walked up.

"Hey," Ivy said. "I think I found the box for the applications. It's over there on the counter."

"Yeah, we already figured that out, thanks," Wren squeaked.

Ivy noticed the look of fear on Amber's face. "What is it?" she asked, glancing around. "Did I miss something?"

With a face so pale that her freckles looked scattered over snow, Amber gulped.

"There are so many applicants," she whispered. "I don't stand a chance. I'll lose. Just like the election. Just like bringing the wrong clothes to sell. I'll lose. There's no point in even turning this stupid flier in."

She tossed the application on the floor, turned, and walked out the door.

11

GREENHOUSE

*P*eople wandered the gray sidewalks along the road back to Wren's house. Amber stared at them silently from the window of her mom's car, going on with their lives, oblivious to her failure. Not caring what a loser she was. *They're all totally selfish*, she told herself. Kammie sat beside her, babbling something, but Amber's ears felt like they were packed with cotton.

Her ears had been that way since she'd walked out of Bespoke. The others followed, separating into the two cars. Wren had to run back inside where Trixie still wandered the racks, not realizing they'd left. *Also selfish*, thought Amber. *She didn't even know I was gone. She's supposed to love me.*

The drive wasn't far. They'd decided to go back to Wren's house to make plans for next week and add their sales money to their treasury box. It was safely tucked away in their workshop, the Greenhouse. At least, the others had decided. Amber just went along with it. It didn't matter anymore.

Amber forced herself to follow Kammie out of the car, oblivious to her mom's goodbye wave as she drove off.

Usually, when Amber came over for club stuff, she used the side gate key all the Renegades had and went directly into Wren's backyard. Today, though, Wren's mom held the door open and they passed right through the small blue Victorian house. Slaloming past boxes, papers, and toys that gathered in piles like snow drifts along the hallway, they made their way to the kitchen in back, then through the sliding glass door to the backyard.

The house was just too small for the four vibrant lives that filled it, but today Amber found herself angry at the mess. She stumbled over a skateboard in the doorway of Trixie and Wren's shared bedroom. *Tripping hazard*, she thought glumly, and kicked the skateboard forcefully back into their room.

Further along the single hallway, the house opened into an inviting kitchen that was usually quite bright — an airlock of sunshine leading from the dark interior to the sun-filled yard beyond.

But today the yard and the kitchen were both dark.

Outside the sliding glass doors, the dreary sky shrouded the house, yard, and their beloved Greenhouse in gray. An overgrown wisteria vine strangled the small, dark shed. Without the lights on, the Greenhouse looked closed for business.

Amber wanted to be home, surrounded by the gauzy

curtains of her four-poster bed, curled under the plush pink bedspread while she squeezed her giant marshmallow-like owl stuffie and disappeared into large shaggy pillows.

Ivy, Wren, and Kammie carried the laundry bags full of her failed attempt to be a hero as if nothing had gone wrong. Together, they headed toward the Greenhouse in the back corner of the yard. No one said anything but their breath came out in little white puffs in the cold.

A pile of Trixie's limbless dolls lay in the middle of the yard. Amber stepped dejectedly over them and pushed her way through the wisteria vine that covered the Greenhouse door. *Wisteria frutescens.* As if it mattered.

It was warm inside. Someone flipped on the light.

The Greenhouse, where the Renegades did their inventing and sciencing, had just been a broken-down old shed when they'd formed their club back in elementary school. Back when it seemed like they had nothing but time, and their most complicated decision was what they wanted for lunch.

Wren's mom had offered to let them use the old greenhouse if they cleaned it up themselves and let Wren's little sister Trixie join the club. The girls had worked tirelessly, cleaning away old spiderwebs and sweeping years of dirt and grime off the floor.

Amber remembered the thrill of watching a usable, private space emerge as they worked together. They'd washed the giant wall of windows, and tightened the screws on the sturdy old potting table. Wren, the handiest with a screwdriver, had reattached broken brackets and straightened the long shelves that lined the back wall from floor to ceiling as they brought the abandoned shed back to life. Over the years, the Renegades had filled those shelves with mishmashed bins full of useful, random stuff: Corrugated cardboard from cut-up shipping boxes; scissors; leftover tiles; sticks; yarn; rolls of different kinds of tape — everything you needed for inventing. They'd all pitched in. Even little Trixie, who had been only 4 years old at the time, had helped wipe, carry, and polish. Amber had carefully pruned the *wisteria frutescens* that first summer.

Though she hadn't touched it since, except to shove it out of the way, the vine had continued to flower and grow. Like their club, like their friendship.

Their prized possession, a beautiful professional-grade microscope, sat on its shelf of honor, secure under a somewhat dusty cover. The microscope had been a gift from Amber's Uncle Tim, who was a microbiologist. When his lab upgraded, the microscope was obsolete technology to him. But to the Renegades, it was like being given the keys to a magic portal, a land filled with microscopic wonder and endless beauty.

At the beginning of the school year, Amber had let it break. A squabble about how Trixie wanted to use some blank slides turned into a scuffle. Wren blamed herself, but Amber knew it was really her fault. She'd managed to catch Trixie, and that should have been the end of it. But she'd failed to hold on to the slippery little eel, who had licked a trail of slime across her arm. It wasn't like Amber to be bothered by a little weaponized tongue. She'd had snakes crawl over her arms and dug beetles out of rotted logs to investigate. But for some reason, Trixie's attack freaked her out that day and the microscope got knocked off the table. The double magnification eyepieces had shattered, and that was that. The microscope was fine. The regular eyepieces still worked with perfectly powerful viewing capacity. But it wasn't the same anymore. Not until they could replace the double magnification eyepieces.

As soon as she shoved through the door, Amber sat heavily on a stool in front of the potting table. The others heaved the bags of discarded clothes into a corner. She barely paid attention, but did notice that Trixie wasn't with them. Somewhere in the back of Amber's mind, she hoped they hadn't left the kid behind after all.

Kammie counted their money, adding it to their treasury.

"Hey, we're getting there!" Kammie's pleasant voice shocked Amber out of her stupor. "That really was a great idea, Amber!"

Amber groaned and dropped her head into her arms.

Ivy rolled her eyes. Wren threw herself onto the table next to Amber's pooling mass of auburn hair.

She poked at Amber's head. "I heard a rumor that there was a person under here!"

Amber swatted the finger away and grumbled, "Go away. My life is over."

"Cut it out, Amber." Ivy's frown deepened. "You're

being dramatic. Firstly, applying for the internship is something you want, so you should do it. The worst they can say is no. Also, it's no big deal if they do say no. You can just make clothes here. Right?"

"I CAN'T," Amber wailed. "Don't you understand? That was it. The deadline! The window closed! I'll never have another chance like that, ever! I messed up. I'm never going to be anybody special. Ever."

Ivy scowled, pulling her phone out. "Look, if you want to do sewing or look at fabric under the microscope or whatever, I'm happy to do that next week. But if we aren't making anything today, I've got to go. I'm behind on some math homework." She paused at the door. "I'm sorry it didn't work out, Amber."

And then she disappeared into the thinning leaves of the wisteria, dialing her mom for a ride home. Amber sniffled as she watched her go.

"Wait, don't go," she said half-heartedly to the closed door. "Oh, what's the point?"

Amber's head sunk back onto the table and her shoulders began to tremble. Her auburn hair shook like a pile of autumn leaves rustling gently in the wind.

"Is anybody there?" Kammie lowered her face to the table and brushed away locks of hair.

"Nobody," Amber whimpered. "I'm nobody."

12

HUMANITY

*S*ocial Studies wasn't Amber's favorite class but it wasn't her least favorite, either. It was just sort of there. Like everything else in life. Flat, blah, unimportant. Nothing seemed important now that she'd lost her chance at the internship.

The class had studied millennia of human civilization in just a few months. From the rise of civilization to the present day. Now they'd arrived at something called globalization.

According to Amber's notes, globalization was "the development of an increasingly integrated global economy, trading freely across national borders and utilizing cheaper foreign labor markets."

According to Amber, globalization was boring.

How else was the world supposed to work? Stuff gets made somewhere, shipped to a store, bought and brought home. She'd never given it much thought beyond noticing all the 'Made in China' stickers on her brother's toys and sometimes trying to guess whether her new leggings came from Bangladesh or Cambodia.

Though honestly she wouldn't be able to pick out Bangladesh or Cambodia on a map. Geography wasn't really her thing. She much preferred geology.

"... and afterwards," her teacher, Mrs. Mailloux, droned on in her cute French accent. "You will write a research paper. This will be an important part of your grade, so I recommend starting early."

Amber looked across the room and tried to catch Ivy's eye, but Ivy was busy paying attention. Amber twirled her pencil on her notebook and glanced at her watch. Class was almost over. Maybe going home would cheer her up.

But Amber hadn't felt cheerful since her weekend of failure. She didn't feel much of anything. She hardly even felt real, like she was watching herself go to school and go home and come to school again, over and over. She felt like a shadow moving through the world, only to disappear, unnoticed, every once in a while, and then reappear, equally unnoticed. But no one else seemed to have even noticed the change in her mood.

Mrs. Mailloux threw out some numbers, and the other kids copied them into their notebooks. Amber didn't listen. If it was important, Ivy would tell her later. Maybe. Or not.

The bell rang. Everyone stood, gathering their books and paper. Amber heaved herself out of her seat, her sloppy loose ponytail flopping against the side of her head, ready to drift silent and unnoticed out the door. Another drop in the sea of other students.

"Amber," Mrs. Mailloux called. "Can you please come see me now?"

She paused. Had she done something wrong? Honestly, she could barely remember the class. She couldn't remember speaking at all, much less saying anything bad. She glanced nervously at Ivy, who hovered in the doorway. Ivy mouthed something Amber couldn't quite make out and, with an apologetic look, swept out the door.

Amber trudged up to the teacher's desk and stood there solemnly. She didn't say anything, just watched the teacher finish up whatever she was working on. Mrs. Mailloux was young, with dark blond hair and wire-framed glasses. Amber watched the pen in her hand bob around as she completed whatever she was writing. After a few seconds, Mrs. Mailloux looked up.

"Amber," the teacher began. Amber paid more attention to her French accent than her words. It was kind of soothing. "I have noticed that you are not being yourself this week. I am concerned. There is perhaps something going on with you of which I should be aware?"

Amber silently shook her head. Mrs. Mailloux couldn't possibly understand. Still, she looked at Amber so kindly. Like she really cared. Amber fidgeted as the teacher waited.

Finally, unable to withstand the gentle stare, she

mumbled, "It's nothing. Nothing at all. It never is. I'm just not special, no matter what I do."

Mrs. Mailloux nodded sagely, straightening the piles on her desk. "I see."

"It's just —" Once Amber started talking, the words spilled out uninvited. "Things were so easy in elementary school, you know? Middle school was supposed to be fun, but so far it sucks. I can't seem to make an impact anywhere. I thought I'd made friends with Gail and Benjamin from eighth grade, but I haven't even seen them since the whole election thing. I keep trying to be great at something, but I'm always just good enough. And this time I didn't even get a chance to try. My best used to mean something. Now, I don't know. I'm just some girl in a fancy dress."

"I think," Mrs. Mailloux steepled her hands as she considered Amber, "you are perhaps someone who has not come up against very many difficulties in life, and sometimes it is quite hard to realize your strength without testing it. Everyone struggles. Sometimes it makes us question ourselves, no?"

Anger crashed through Amber's quiet fog. Not many difficulties? Question herself? What did this woman even know about her? What did she even mean about being herself anyway?

Amber looked down at her outfit. No fancy dress today, that was true. But her sweatpants had been so soft and fluffy when she'd worn them to bed last night with the plain, simple sweater. She just hadn't bothered to change.

Okay, that was pretty uncharacteristic. But that didn't mean anything. It certainly didn't mean she'd never faced any difficulties. Did it?

The teacher was watching her face as the anger started to give way to confusion.

"Amber," she offered quietly. "Have you heard of the Power of Yet, yet?"

"Ummmm. No?"

"I find when I am stuck on the problem, and do not know what to do," Mrs. Mailloux continued, standing and gathering her purse and jacket, "it is helpful for me to say my problem, and add the word 'yet' at the end. Just, simply 'yet.'"

Amber scoffed. "Seriously?"

"*Mais oui*, Amber. Seriously. It is indeed very serious power. Do promise me you will give it a try, no?" Mrs. Mailloux grinned at her, moving out from behind her desk. "We both need to go now. I have much to do for the next week, and I do not know how I will get it all done. Yet."

Amber shifted her books and headed towards the door with the teacher.

"And Amber," Mrs. Mailloux added. "I always enjoy your lovely clothings. I hope they return along with your smile."

Amber smiled politely and headed to her locker.

Add 'yet' to the end of a problem. What a stupid idea.

13

SURPRISE!

*A*mber's bedroom door crashed open. Blaise dashed inside and slammed it shut. Someone pounded on it from the outside.

"NO WAY, AIDEN!" Blaise screamed at the door, bracing it closed with his wiry little body.

Amber lay face down and despondent on her fluffy bed among dozens of delicate dresses, pants, and shirts. She still hadn't put them away from the day she'd worn her beloved lilac Carpaccio. The day she'd been filled with hope. Before everything had come crashing down. Now she lay drowning in a sea of beautiful fabric, wearing the same sweatpants and cozy shirt she'd been wearing for days.

"Get out, you butthead," Amber mumbled into the pink velvet comforter.

"My head's not a butt," Blaise spit back, then laughed at his own joke. He looked like a gangly puppy, all ears and big hands and feet hanging off a lanky body. Gigantic brown eyes shone with life under a head of strawberry blonde hair that was so short and thick it looked like fur.

The door cracked open, knocking him off balance. He threw his body against it again with hysterical laughter and pushed the lock. The doorknob rattled violently and the thudding started again.

From the other side a voice, cracking with puberty, howled, "LET ME IN! Now!"

Amber rolled over to face the wall. On her polished white desk, her glittering Italian backpack slouched open. All her homework remained untouched inside.

"You're not allowed in here, Blaise," Amber told the wall. "I didn't give you permission to come in here."

Blaise ignored her. The hammering continued against the door. Amber groaned in exasperation.

"MOOOOOM! THE BOYS WON'T LEAVE ME ALONE!"

"Boys," a muffled, barely audible reply came from downstairs, "leave your sister alone."

"MOOOOOM!" Amber groaned, rolling onto her back and flopping a hand over her eyes. "Come on."

Blaise flung open the door. Aiden, lurking outside, grabbed at him. They both thundered away down the hall.

"And stay out," Amber moaned, slamming the door and locking it this time. She flopped down in her desk chair and yanked a book out of her backpack at random. It was on globalization. She tossed it down, unopened, and crawled back to bed.

The doorknob jiggled. Blaise hammered against it, desperately screaming, "AMBER!"

The pounding stopped and she heard feet running again.

"AMBER!" came another call through the door. But it wasn't one of her brothers this time. It was her mom.

Amber dragged herself to the door and opened it. "Yeah?"

"Come down here, honey," her mom yelled excitedly. "You'll want to see this."

"BUT," Amber stared dumbfounded at the computer screen. "I didn't even turn in the application. I mean, I kind of threw it on the floor."

"Apparently someone found it." Her mom pointed to the email.

It was crystal clear. And it had obviously been sent to the correct person. Amber looked at her mom in confusion and read the email out loud again.

"Dear Amber Rosenberg, congratulations. We are pleased to inform you that you have been chosen to be a finalist for the youth internship position at Bespoke Custom Clothiers. You are one of seven lucky contestants who will compete in the Fashion Face-Off. Please find the contest rules below. If you have any further questions, please do not hesitate to contact us. We look forward to seeing your designs. Best Regards, Bespoke Custom Clothiers." Amber turned to her mom. "I'm not going to read all that stuff at the bottom, but I still don't understand."

"Hey!" Her mom reached over from where she sat in front of the computer and hugged Amber's waist. "All your dreams are coming true! Great job! This is..." She paused, looking her daughter up and down. "Wait, aren't those your pajamas? Did you wear that to school today?"

"Could be," Amber shrugged.

"Well, I hope you'll at least change your underwear before you go to bed tonight."

"Mooooom!"

"Really, honey, this is fabulous," her mom continued. "Let's celebrate with a girls' day out! I'll book us some appointments at the hair stylist and we can go shopping! Maybe we can even find you something special to wear to your show here. Something a little more appropriate than pajamas."

Amber didn't answer.

"Honey?"

"Oh, yes," Amber snapped back to herself and smiled. "That sounds great."

"I'll go make some calls and get us booked." Her mom's heels clicked on the hardwood floor as she left the room.

Amber watched her go. This was it. What she wanted more than anything. What she'd dreamed about. It was finally happening for her. So why wasn't she more excited? Why did she suddenly feel like she might throw up?

14

SLEEVES

*T*rixie munched on her jelly sandwich, watching her mom wrap yarn around some knitting needles. The big girls were already in the Greenhouse. She wanted to join them but Mom was making her finish this stupid sandwich first. This stupid, delicious sandwich.

Suddenly, through the sliding glass doors, Trixie heard noise in the yard. Screams. Her head shot up. Screaming, yelling. Somebody was in trouble.

She tossed her crusts onto the table next to her plate and rushed to the door. Pressing her face and hands against the glass, she peered out across the yard into the Greenhouse. Purple jelly smeared between her skin and the door. Across the yard and through the windows of the Greenhouse, the big girls jumped like the floor was on fire or they had ants in their shoes. Her sister popped onto the potting table and waved her arms around while the others clung to Amber. They kept screaming.

They were clearly in trouble. Behind her, Mom played with her knitting needles and yarn, oblivious. It was up to her.

She had to save them.

Trixie pulled her gooey hands from the glass door with a wet squelch and slid it open, rocketing across the small yard, leaving her handprints and an open door behind. The wisteria had lost most of its leaves, but the ropy vines were still between her and the big girls. Trixie yanked a branch aside and tumbled through the door.

"What is it?" Trixie panted. "Are you okay? Is it ants? Fire? Ants on fire?"

To her surprise, the Renegades smiled. Amber swept Trixie into her arms and spun them both around.

"Amber got an eeeemaaaaail," Wren sang, wiggling her butt in a weird little dance.

Trixie didn't see what was so exciting about an email, but Amber was hugging her, so she didn't really care. Trixie hugged her back, letting go only when the redhead finally set her down.

"I'm in the contest, Trixie! The Fashion Face-Off!" Amber's face was glowing, but Trixie thought she heard a little bit of hesitation in her voice.

"You're taking your face off for fashion?" It sounded painful. Maybe that's why they were screaming.

"No," Ivy told her. "It's the fashion contest for that internship at Bespoke. I have to admit, I'm kind of excited about making fashions. I mean, I don't want to be an intern, but I'm always up for a challenge. Another chance for the Renegades to triumph!"

"You really should stay closer to your mom," Kammie told Trixie firmly. "You know you scared everyone when you disappeared at the store last weekend."

"Mom says I'm an adventure," Trixie nodded. "How do you make clothes?"

"It's so fun!" Amber replied. "You'll see."

"Okay," Trixie shrugged. "Do you need yarn? Mom has yarn! I'll get some for you."

And before they could stop her, Trixie ran back out of the Greenhouse. Amber wiped at the sticky residue on her shirt as she watched her disappear.

"I love the clothes you make," Kammie added. "How DO you do it?"

"Yeah," Wren grabbed a shirt from Amber's bag and flattened it on the potting table. "How do you make flat fabric into something that fits around a round body and doesn't look like you just wrapped a towel around yourself?"

"It's really interesting," Amber gushed. "Sewing is sort of like a floppy puzzle. The shapes you cut out of fabric look like big puzzle pieces. Once you stitch them together, they become whole new shapes. Shapes you can wear."

"What's interesting about it?" Ivy asked. "I mean, it can't be that complicated. You sew some cylinders together and you're done."

Amber smirked. She handed Ivy a marker and pointed

to Trixie's old art easel. "Draw what you think a shirt would look like taken apart."

"Well," Ivy sketched as she spoke. "I'd expect it to be a long rectangle for the sleeve, attached to a square with a neck hole in it for the body. And of course another rectangle on the other side for the other sleeve."

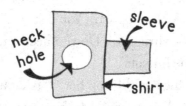

"Sorry, but would that really work?" Kammie squinted at the drawing. "What happens when you move your arm down?"

"Exactly," Amber nodded. "The fabric would pull off your shoulder and bunch up in your armpit."

Wren snorted. "The way you sweat, Ivy, a whole bunch of fabric wadded into your armpit would be disgusting!"

"But. I mean," Ivy rubbed the back of her neck thought-fully. "How else do you do it?"

"Find out," Amber picked the shirt up from the table and turned it inside out. She tossed it to Ivy. "Cut that apart."

Ivy caught the shirt and raised an eyebrow. "Cut it? Why?"

"Trust me." Amber handed her some heavy scissors.

"Just cut along the seams. You'll see the shapes it's really made out of."

Ivy grabbed the scissors with a shrug, snipping along the side seam. It went in one long L-shaped line from the hem at the bottom of the shirt all the way up past the armpit and out to the wrist cuff of the sleeve.

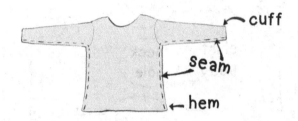

With the sleeve still attached, she spread the shirt open on the table. Unlike her drawing, the opened shirt wouldn't lay flat. It bubbled up where the sleeve met the body, right where her shoulder would go.

"That's weird."

Wren poked at the bubble. "Cut the sleeve off. I want to see what shape it is."

Ivy snipped through the rounded seam on the shoulder. Two pieces fell away; the sleeve, which was actually curved and had a funny bump at the top, and the body of the shirt, which was actually two pieces sewn together between the shoulder and then neck hole. The place the sleeve had been attached looked like a big C.

Ivy drew the shapes on the easel's paper.

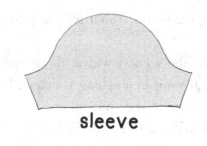

sleeve

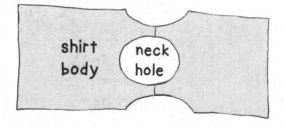

shirt
body   neck
hole

"The sleeve looks like a pirate hat!" Wren wiggled her fingers for the marker. "I'm gonna draw a skull and cross-bones on it!"

"No," Amber pushed her hand away. "I'm making a point here."

"Arrrg, matey!" Wren drawled, squinting one eye. "I'll keelhaul ya, scalawag! Ye'll walk the plank fer shore!"

"Be serious." Ivy tried to fit the sleeve back in the curve of the shirt's body. They didn't line up exactly. "So, these curves make the sleeve bump up over the shoulder, but tuck in at the armpit? That's some really complicated geometry. I can't imagine the kind of math that goes into those measurements."

"Yup," Amber nodded. "Granny and I always use

premade patterns for sleeves, even if we're inventing the rest of the outfit. You can get really fancy with sleeves. You can use more fabric, then gather it up again so it poofs out, like a princess sleeve. You can make it huge and baggy, which changes the shoulder shape a lot. You can make all sorts of different sleeves, like raglan or batwing sleeves, or use a yoke."

"I don't understand those words," Kammie whispered.

Amber shrugged. "It's just words we use in sewing for different pattern pieces. But these curvy type sleeves are used in most clothes. The ones that look..."

"Like a pirate hat, me hearty," Wren interrupted. "Avast!"

"...ALL CURVY." Amber glared at Wren as she talked over her. "Sleeves have changed a lot throughout history. They're one of the easiest ways to see what era a movie is supposed to be from. Like in Romeo and Juliet times, they'd actually make two sleeves on top of each other and cut a slit in the top one. Then they'd puff the bottom one through the cuts! But all sleeves have to solve the problem of the shoulder area. It moves so much in all different directions!"

"I wonder how they deal with the shoulders on a space-suit," Kammie pondered.

"No idea," Amber tapped her lips thoughtfully. "That's an interesting question."

"Yargh," Wren drawled. "What about a pair o'knickers, lassie?"

Everyone just stared at her. Wren shook her head sadly

and dug a pair of leggings out of Amber's bag. "You guys need to watch more pirate movies."

"Oh! Pants! They're fascinating too!" Amber flipped the pants inside out. "Here, cut these up."

She held out the leggings to Kammie. Amber let go, thinking Kammie was holding them, but they fell onto the table.

"I can't cut up perfectly good clothes," Kammie cried, refusing to touch them.

"Of course you can." Amber thrust the scissors at her. "Just use the scissors. It's no big deal, they're already falling apart."

"But what if I mess it up?" moaned Kammie.

"It's got HOLES! You literally CAN'T mess it up." Amber pointed to some tiny holes near the seam.

Kammie took the scissors with two fingers and looked at them like they were covered in boogers.

"Cutting clothes is WRONG," Kammie mumbled to herself. "And wasteful."

"I like the word scalawag," added Wren.

"Stop talking pirate!" Amber laughed.

"Aye, matey." Wren grabbed a marker and snuck over to Ivy's sleeve drawing.

The door opened.

"Mom wouldn't share," said a trembling voice from outside. "But she said I had to."

Trixie's arms overflowed with yarn. She had a book with a redheaded woman on the cover. Setting the book on a nearby shelf, she dumped the yarn right on top of the cut-up shirt.

Ivy picked up a yellow ball of yarn. A big red sticker on the label said CLEARANCE. All the yarn had LAST CHANCE and SALE stickers, but other than that, they were completely different from one another. The canary yellow one bumped into a huge, fluffy, brownish ball that looked like a rope made of gerbils. A knot of what looked like silver embroidery floss lay under the gerbil rope. Near it, some unpleasant salmony pink yarn nestled against some wubby purple twine.

It was Trixie's birthday stash.

"For us?" Amber asked, reaching for the pile.

"SHARING. Not giving," Trixie scowled. She shoved the sickly pink ball at Amber, then hugged the purple one possessively.

Ivy suddenly dropped the sleeve. Wren looked up from the skull she was drawing on the easel.

"Is this...?" Ivy reached for the silvery floss with wide eyes. It looked like thick sewing thread. "Oh WOW. Where did you FIND this?"

"At the art store," Trixie said in an exaggeratedly slow voice. "Remember? You were there."

"It is! Look! LOOK!!" Ivy shook the thread at the others. No one said anything. The thread wasn't even particularly pretty. It was just sort of a dull gray. She shook it at them again and, not getting a satisfactory response, finally yelled, "Guys, this is CONDUCTIVE THREAD!"

"Shiver me timbers!" gasped Wren.

"Right?" Excitement radiated from Ivy's usually serious face.

"Actually, I have no idea what you're talking about," Wren clarified. "But I'm here to support you."

Ivy groaned. "Here, I'll show you."

She grabbed a bin marked ELECTRONIC STUFF and dug out a button battery and a tiny light made of a plastic dome and two metal legs sticking out from the bottom. One leg was shorter than the other.

"That's an LED, right?" Amber asked. Ivy, who wanted to be an electrical engineer like her mom, often used the small lights. "You use that little battery to light it up?"

"Right, a light-emitting diode. LED." Ivy straddled the legs of the LED around the battery, one leg touching each side. Nothing happened, so she flipped the battery around. As soon as the legs touched the new sides of the battery, the dome lit up brightly. "It's a simple circuit. The electricity goes out one side of the battery, up the leg, into the bulb, down the other leg, and back into the battery, like a circle. But the legs have to be on the correct sides of the battery for it to work. I can use this, right Trixie?"

Ivy held scissors to the thread, looking beseechingly at the younger girl.

"I'm sharing," Trixie whispered, clutching the gerbil rope possessively against her chest.

"Thanks!" Ivy cut two pieces, wrapping one around each leg. Then she folded the legs so the thread wouldn't fall off. She set the LED on the table and, keeping the threads from touching each other, pressed one thread to each side of the battery. The light lit up again. "The thread is like a wire, it's conductive, meaning the electricity can move through it. But unlike a wire, it's really flexible."

Amber stared silently at the light. "You can...SEW...with that?"

Ivy grinned. "Now you see why I was so excited. Just think of all the possibilities for your fashions!"

Amber gingerly touched the circuit in Ivy's hands.

"I can think of about twenty ways to use lights on an outfit right now. This is gonna be fun." Amber stood up straight, her hazel eyes glowing, and declared, "Let's get down to business!"

sleeve

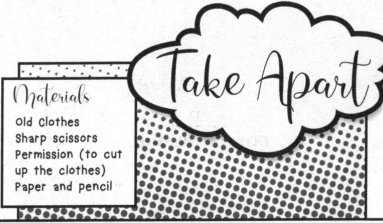

Take Apart

Materials

Old Clothes
Sharp scissors
Permission (to cut up the clothes)
Paper and pencil

Clothes are made of pieces sewn together like a cloth puzzle. Draw what you think the pieces look like before they're sewn.

Turn the clothes inside out. The places clothes are sewn together are called SEAMS.

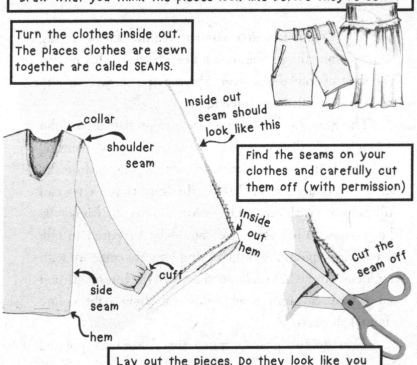

Inside out seam should look like this

collar

shoulder seam

Find the seams on your clothes and carefully cut them off (with permission)

Inside out hem

cuff

Cut the seam off

side seam

hem

Lay out the pieces. Do they look like you thought? Can you put them back together? Can you make something else with them?

15

DOWN TO BUSINESS

*E*veryone looked at Amber. Waiting for her to say something. She took a deep breath. This was it. The start of something great. She taped a printout of the email to the wall and pointed to it.

"The rules are, I have four weeks to prepare a portfolio of four to eight designs. I can have help," she read, pointing to them, "from my wonderful friends, as long as I do the actual designing myself. I think that means you guys can still help me with ideas. Um, we can have our friends be the models. What else? We should be prepared to talk about our inspirations and why and how we came up with our ideas. And what we hope to do with the internship and our future. So, four weeks puts the show right before Hanukkah starts."

"That doesn't give us much time," Kammie pointed out.

"True." Amber tapped her lips. "Let's double up on the

weekends. Saturday AND Sunday from now until the contest."

Wren shrugged indifferently, and Trixie nodded happily, but Ivy and Kammie looked at each other.

"I have my last soccer game of the season tomorrow, Amber," Ivy said. "It's super important. And the team is having a pizza party afterwards. Kammie was going to go with me."

Amber frowned. "But this is important."

Ivy sighed. "I'll try to stop by afterwards, but I really don't know how long it will take. Kammie, you don't have to come if you want to be here instead, I guess."

Kammie's eyes got wide. She looked from Ivy to Amber. "I don't know what to do. It's the last game. What should I do?"

"Both!" Trixie offered enthusiastically. "Do everything!"

"But..." Kammie hesitated.

Ivy put a hand on her shoulder. "It's okay. I can get a ride from one of the other girls on the team. I'd love to have you there, but it's okay."

"All right." Kammie nodded uncertainly. "I guess I can come then."

"And after today, I get a few weeks off before basket-ball ramps up," Ivy offered. "So I should be able to join you guys unless I have a big school project or something."

"Sounds good." Wren clapped her hands together and rubbed them vigorously. "What are we going to tinker up, Captain Amber?"

"That's Science Princess Amber, thank you!" She thrust

her nose up in the air. "But you may call me Your Science Highness."

"Dream on." Wren threw a piece of cardboard at her.

"A brainstorming session is in order." Amber handed Kammie a marker and gestured elegantly toward the easel where Ivy's sleeve drawing now had a skull and crossbones on it.

Kammie pulled a fresh sheet of butcher paper over it.

"I remember brainstorming!" yelled Trixie. "Kammie writes down all our ideas, even weird stuff. Then we pick the best ones."

"Yup!" Ivy settled onto a stool. "Where do we start?"

"What's the problem?" Wren replied, pointing to another paper taped to the wall. It said *Engineering Design Process*.

Discovering the process had been a turning point for Wren. Following a structure helped her organize and stay focused on a task. With a little structure, Wren was learning how to channel her crazy, creative, divergent thinking into powerful problem-solving.

The first step of the Engineering Design Process was the question *What's the Problem?* Defining the problem wasn't always as easy as it seemed.

After that, it went into a cycle of *Imagine, Create, Test, Evaluate,* and back to *Imagine.* Then they were supposed to *Share the Results.* They didn't always do every step in the process but it was still helpful.

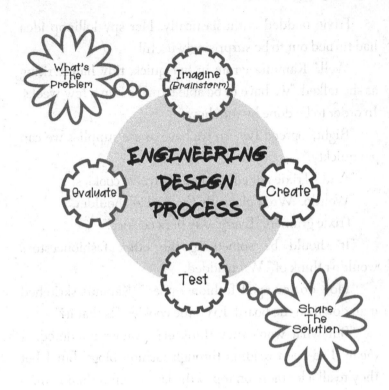

"Here's the problem," Amber sighed. "How do I compete with older, more fashion-forward, totally cool kids?"

"Right now, the problem is your bad attitude," Ivy quipped. "Anything worth doing is going to be hard."

"The *PROBLEM*," Wren corrected, "is figuring out what sorts of fashion stuff we're going to kick butt with. What can we make that nobody else will? Maybe if we list our strengths and limitations we can come up with a bunch of ideas. Right? It worked for our spy gear."

Trixie nodded enthusiastically. Her spy lollipop idea had turned out to be surprisingly useful.

"Well," Kammie wrote in her quick, tidy handwriting as she talked, "we have to be able to make it in a few weeks. In order to be done by the show."

"Right," agreed Ivy, "so we have to use supplies we can get quickly."

"And," Trixie added, "it should involve cookies!"

"Weirdo." Wren playfully shoved her shoulder.

Trixie grinned. "Everybody likes cookies!"

"It should be something the other fashioneestoes wouldn't think of," Wren added.

"How do you spell 'fashioneestoes'?" Kammie skritched it all down on the board. Even the cookies. "Is that it?"

"But what won't they think of?" Amber pondered. "I mean, I've been reading through fashion blogs, but I bet they're all a lot more on top of the latest trends than I am."

"Maybe," Wren shrugged. "But I bet none of them know the genus and species name of cotton."

"*Gossypium hirsutum*," Amber replied. "But I don't know how that can help us."

"Except, it can, right?" Wren said. "One thing we have that they probably don't is all our tinkering."

"Yes," Ivy agreed. "We should use our strengths."

Amber slowly nodded. "Well, I do want to use that conductive thread and sew a circuit in something."

Trixie grabbed the yarn on the table. "Can we do yarn?"

Kammie paused. "Make yarn or use yarn?"

"Both!" Trixie exclaimed excitedly. "Mom is using lots of yarn. She tried to teach me finger knitting but she isn't a very good teacher."

"Yeah," Wren agreed. "She can make a lot of stuff but sucks at explaining. She's not really the most patient person."

Trixie nodded.

"What else?" Kammie asked. "Maybe we can use patterns. Oh! How about beads? You can make really cool designs with colored beads."

She wrote it all down.

"Maybe we could make our own beads from bioplastic. That was really fun." Amber looked over the list thoughtfully. "Hmmm, but what KINDS of stuff? There's more to a good outfit than just the clothing. Shirts, dresses, and pants, sure, but also shoes, jewelry, hair accessories, stuff like that."

Kammie listed each item and added "socks."

"How do you make shoes?" Wren looked doubtful.

"We can sort through it later," Ivy waved off the question. "Any other ideas?"

They started at each other blankly.

"I can't think of anything else," Wren shrugged. "This seemed a lot easier when we brainstormed spy gear."

"With spy stuff we thought about the Sarah and Simon books," Trixie reminded them. "Dad just finished reading me *The Morocco Mystery* last night. Their fashion style was mostly clothes with lots of pockets."

"That's true, we had inspiration." Wren remembered

how enthusiastically they'd all called out ideas while thinking about what a spy would need. "But I haven't read any inspirational books on teenage fashion designers who save the world from evil fashion agents."

"Wow." Amber's eyes lit up. "I'd LOVE to read that!"

"But books like that don't exist," Wren frowned. "I just said that."

"You're the boss here, Amber." Ivy crossed her arms. "What sorts of projects can you think of with these ideas?"

"Okay." Amber got serious. "We need a few specific ideas to get us started. Refine what ideas we do have. Let's see. Maybe we can put the sewn circuit on some kind of accessory once we get it to work. Like a necklace or a purse. Beads are a good idea. And not just for jewelry. We could bead something unusual, like fingerless gloves or something. I like the idea of making our own yarn. We could weave it into fabric. No one else would have anything like that. And..." she glanced at Trixie, "I bet we can think of something really cool to do with a long finger-knit chain! Can anybody handle that job?"

"Oh me!" Trixie yelled excitedly waving her hand in the air. "Me!"

"Oh, you'd be perfect!" Amber gasped. "Why didn't I think of that?"

Kammie organized all their ideas into columns.

Strengths & Limitations	Ideas	KINDS of Stuff	Refined Ideas
Make in a few weeks	Sewn Circuit	Shirts	**Sewn Circuit** -accessory -necklace -purse
Easy to get supplies	Make Yarn	Dresses	
Cookies	Use Yarn	Pants	**Beads** -jewelry -gloves
Something other ~~fashini~~ ~~fashinee~~ **contestants** won't think of	Finger Knit	Shoes	
	Patterns -beads?	Jewelry	**Yarn** -weave fabric -finger knit
		Hair Accessories	
Tinkering		Socks	Beading Patterns

They stared at the lists. They weren't exactly the sort of well-thought-out, detailed lists they had made for their spy project. They were sloppy and kind of random.

"Hmmm. Brainstorming is a lot easier with some inspiration," Amber sighed. "But it's enough to get started, anyway. We can add to the lists and sort them as we go, but it's a good first step. Gotta start somewhere. So, for tomorrow. Kammie, use our bead bin to make something beady. Wren, can you tinker up some yarn? I have no idea how to DIY yarn, but it sounds right up your alley. And Ivy and I can work on the sewn circuit."

Trixie sat patiently watching Amber, waiting for her

assignment. Amber hesitated. She had forgotten all about her.

"And Trixie!" Amber added. "You have the most important job of all. Are you ready?"

Trixie nodded vigorously.

"I want you to make the longest, prettiest, best finger knit ever. But it has to be really good. Can you do that?"

Trixie held up her wad of yarn with determination. "I will! The best ever! As soon as I learn how."

"Alright!" Wren yelled, throwing a fist in the air dramatically. "Let's start strong tomorrow. Let's show these people what the Renegades can do! Let's science the heck out of this Fashion Face-Off."

16

PATTERNS

"*I* just want to DO something!," Amber griped on Sunday. "Ivy is so late, and I can't start the circuit without her help."

She'd already gathered a bunch of supplies, straightened the Greenhouse, and prepared everything to get started.

"I don't think her game is over yet," Kammie offered. "Remember?"

"Sure, but we don't have a ton of time to wait around." Amber flopped on a stool. The book Trixie had brought in yesterday caught her attention. She swiped it off the shelf and began paging through it impatiently. Wren leaned back against the wall of windows, her stool balanced on two legs, as she poked at an iPad. Amber glared at her, watching her mess with the screen, but turned back to the book without saying anything. At least Kammie was actually working.

Kammie looked down at her bin labeled 'LITTLE ROUND THINGS' and the plastic working tray next to it. She'd decided to start with a necklace.

Buttons, beads, weird Canadian coins, and plastic rings filled the bin, encased in mint tins, glass baby food jars, and baggies. She took out tons of beads in all different sizes, materials, and colors. Elastic cord, scissors, fishing line, and thread soon joined her pile. She was ready to get started.

The pile of supplies stared up at her.

She stared back.

Now what?

She tried to imagine a necklace pattern out of the mess of beads in front of her. Patterns were beautiful and soothing. Predictable. The beads in front of her were chaotic. Intimidating. She looked away from the pile in frustration. Couldn't she even get started? It seemed like such a big task.

Next to her, Trixie looked pretty frustrated too. The girl had yarn tangled all over her sticky little fingers. She tugged at the knotted yarn, fighting back tears. She kept trying to pull it over the same finger, but it wouldn't budge. Her finger was red and starting to swell.

"Looks like you have a bug in your program," Kammie observed.

"A BUG? Where?" Trixie squealed. She shook her hand, yanking frantically at the yarn.

"Sorry! Not a real bug." Kammie gently took Trixie's hand and started to loosen the yarn. "That was a dumb thing to say. I just mean your program isn't running right."

"Program? What program?" Trixie asked as Kammie pulled the yarn from her fingers.

"A program, like on a computer. It's just an expression. A program is instructions about how to do something. You write the code to tell the computer what to do, then it follows your instructions."

"But this is YARN." Trixie looked at her like she was crazy.

"A program can be anything." Kammie began untangling the yarn. "They can tell you how to do all kinds of stuff, even finger knitting. The basic ideas behind any program are pretty simple by themselves, but when you put them together, they can do really powerful things."

"I can't do really powerful things," Trixie moped.

"Of course you can." Wren looked up from her iPad and chuckled. "You're tough, Trix. You can do it."

Trixie took the unknotted yarn from Kammie. "You think so?"

"I know so," Wren smirked. "Nobody is more annoying than you when you decide to do something."

Trixie laughed. "You are."

Wren stuck out her tongue and turned back to her iPad.

"With a little structure, you'd be surprised at how much you can do. Even me, and I'm not a very good programmer." Kammie held up her hand, palm towards Trixie, and spread out her fingers. "Go like this."

"You're not?" Trixie mirrored Kammie's hand.

"Well, I LIKE it. I like writing code. But I'm not like a

hacker. I'm not even the best in my class. Ivy's in my coding class and she does pretty well."

"Ivy does pretty well at everything," Wren mumbled to her iPad.

"But you don't have to be the best at something to enjoy it." Kammie put the tail of the yarn in the little U between Trixie's thumb and fingers. "Hold that with your thumb."

"Why?" asked Trixie, pressing her thumb against the yarn to keep it in place. "Why keep doing something you're not good at."

"Well, I didn't say I wasn't ANY good," Kammie replied defensively. "I'm not bad or anything. I bet your dad wasn't a good programmer when he started learning either, and now he makes video games."

Trixie thought about that. "So, what do you like about it?"

Kammie considered the question while she wove the yarn in between Trixie's fingers. She went in front of the index finger, behind the middle finger, in front of the ring finger, and wrapped it around behind the pinky finger, then did the opposite on the way back to her thumb. Now each finger had a thread in front of it and behind it, crossing between the fingers.

"I like the idea of solving a problem, but when I'm faced with one, I don't know how to start. It's overwhelming. Like with these beads." Kammie glanced at the pile of chaotic colors and sizes. "But with code, there are specific steps to take. The ideas are simple, and everything's logical. I like to break big goals down into little steps, and do them one by one. That's exactly what a program does. It's just a series of instructions to solve a problem."

"That makes sense, I guess." Trixie turned her hand flat as Kammie laid the yarn across her fingers, above the wrapped yarn, so the new yarn was closer to her fingertips.

"It does!" Kammie agreed. "That's the point. Code makes sense. It's not wishy-washy. It can't be. Computers need really specific instructions. Anybody can write code once they learn the rules."

"And my yarn is a code?" Trixie tried to lift her hand to look at the yarn more closely, but Kammie held it in place.

"Do you remember those structures I told you about? The simple little ideas that make up instructions? You can use them for anything. A sequence, a loop, and a selection. Like this, we can start with a sequence. Fold." Kammie folded Trixie's index finger down to cover the new bit of yarn. "Tuck." She lifted the wrapped yarn from the bottom of the index finger and gently inserted Trixie's fingertip underneath. "Pull." She pulled the yarn loop lightly over Trixie's bent knuckle until it rested on the back of her hand. "That's a sequence. A list of stuff in a particular order. One after another. Once you figure out your sequence, you can loop it."

Trixie watched Kammie fold, tuck, and pull on her other three fingers. "Loop?"

"Yeah, a loop is where you do the same thing, like the commands in a sequence, over and over again until you're done." Kammie opened Trixie's fingers and laid more yarn over them. Then she folded, tucked, and pulled the yarn over each finger going the other way, from her pinky to her index finger.

"When are you done?" Trixie tentatively reached out to try it herself.

"Well, that's up to you," Kammie shrugged. "You just have to keep asking yourself if your finger-knit chain is long enough. Which is like the third idea, a selection. In programming, we call it an if/then statement. You ask a question to figure out which path to follow next. In this case, you could ask, 'Do I like my finger-knit chain?' If you do, great, you're done. Tie it off. If you don't, you can make it longer, or switch the color, or whatever."

"That's what coding is? That doesn't seem so hard." Trixie suddenly realized one of her fingers didn't have any yarn around it at all. "AGH! I'm a bad programmer! I made a bug!"

"No! No," Kammie reassured her. "Every programmer gets bugs. That's just part of the process. Just find the bug, figure out why it's not working, and fix it."

Trixie took a deep breath. She traced the yarn and found where she'd accidentally pulled both strands over her knuckle. "I guess I didn't fold my finger right. But look! If I pull this over like this, I fixed it! Look! I fixed it!"

"Look at you go." Kammie pointed to the chain that was already building.

Trixie smiled. "It's easier for me to remember what to do when it's only a few steps over and over. And that way it's not so scary to start."

"Right?" Kammie turned back to her beads. "I wish I could code a necklace."

"Why can't you?" Trixie asked. "If you make up a sequence of beads, and loop them, wouldn't that make a nice necklace pattern?"

"That's true!" Kammie agreed. "Right now I don't even know how many of each kind of bead I have, though. But how should I group them? By size, weight, color, or material?"

Trixie started shoving the beads around. "Let's sort them by size, then by color! I love sorting."

Kammie watched with amazement as Trixie quickly made 3 piles — small, medium, and large. It seemed so easy when she only concentrated on one category at a time. She didn't pay attention to anything but their size. Then Kammie helped her sort each pile into rainbow order.

It was beautiful. Everything where it belonged. Kammie could have hugged Trixie.

Just then, Amber looked up from the book. "Hey Trixie, where did you get this book?"

"Huh?" she looked over. "Oh! I got it from Mom's sewing pile. It was the only one with fashion clothes. Do you like it? The pictures looked pretty. I like the lady, she looks like you grown up. It's too hard for me to read, so I don't know what it's about."

On the cover of the book, an older woman with gray-streaked red hair piled on her head was dressed in a mish-mash of red plaids and black-and-white stripes.

"It's about a designer named Vivienne Westwood."

Amber pointed to the woman on the cover. "I've never seen anything like these fashions! Talk about a renegade."

Amber drifted back into the book while Kammie looked at her beads.

After a little trial and error, she found a pattern sequence she was happy with: small blue, medium purple, large red, two medium blues, small red, small purple. She measured a length of fishing wire and tied a large yellow bead to the end to keep all the other beads from falling off, then threaded them in that order again and again and again. So much work! But it was the kind of calming, simple, repetitive work that Kammie found soothing. Wren hated this kind of work, but having different skills and interests made them a good team. They could really help each other.

She held up the finished piece and admired it.

"That looks really nice," Trixie said, dangling the strand between Wren and her iPad screen. "Look, Wrenny. Isn't it pretty?"

"It's fabulous! Nice job. Amber will totally win with stuff like this," Wren smiled. "Hey Trix, I bet you're going to miss Amber when she's big and famous."

"What do you mean?" Trixie scowled.

"When she gets this internship, Amber's going to be busier than Ivy!" Wren teased loudly, so Amber could hear. "She won't have time for boring people like us anymore."

Amber laughed.

"What? Nuh-uh! Really?" Trixie gasped. "If I knew

that, I would never have put your stupid paper away in the box."

"Wait," Amber closed the book, staring at her. "YOU turned in the application?"

"It was on the floor," Trixie explained.

"So THAT'S why you disappeared in the store," Wren smacked herself on the forehead. "I didn't think any of those other kids would have turned in a competitor's application."

"But are you leaving, Amber?" Trixie asked.

"I was only kidding," Wren soothed. "Amber's stuck with us whether she likes it or not."

Trixie turned pleading eyes to Amber. "Really?"

"Of course I'm not going anywhere. The internship may only be for one person, but we're a team!" But it was true, Amber thought to herself. An internship would take up a lot of time. She hadn't even considered what sorts of hours she'd have to work.

Why was everything so complicated? Once you got what you wanted, you were supposed to get your happy ending, right? They all lived happily ever after. You weren't supposed to have to keep working at your happily ever after once all your dreams came true.

Outside, the wisteria rustled suddenly. Amber had been too distracted to see anyone coming. The door creaked open and Ivy trudged in. She wore a clean t-shirt but still smelled like sweat.

"How did it go?" Kammie perked up. "Did you win?"

Ivy frowned and sat heavily on a nearby stool.

"Soooo," Wren began. "Not so good?"

"It was the last game of the season! Not enough hustle." Ivy crossed her arms angrily. "Mom's waiting in the driveway to head to the pizza party. I'm just stopping by to check in and let Kammie know everybody wants you to come. You're sort of unofficially part of the team since you come to almost all the games."

"Yes!" Kammie began to pack away her beads excitedly.

"But we have so much work to do!" Amber looked frantically at them. "Ivy and I haven't even started the circuit! I can't do it by myself, I don't know how."

Kammie paused. "But I'm done for now. I really want to go. Please? They're my friends too."

"We'll have to work extra hard next weekend." Amber looked around her carefully arranged work area as Kammie finished cleaning up. Her eyes fell on her watch. Mom would come pick her up in a few minutes. Where had the time gone? "I guess it's time to go anyway. Let's make sure to close the door tightly so nothing happens to what we HAVE managed to get done."

"What could happen to it? Look..." Wren waved her iPad at them. "I've been doing research on making yarn. I can try it during the week so it'll be ready to go next weekend."

Ivy held the door open for Kammie. "Look, Amber, I can come over after school to work on the circuit with you, okay? I think I can squeeze in some time Tuesday afternoon."

Then they were gone, running toward the side gate,

leaving Amber, Wren, and Trixie alone. As they disappeared around the corner, Amber felt a sudden chill.

What if they couldn't get done in time? What if she went to the contest against all those high schoolers with half-finished, slapped together designs? Suddenly, Amber realized what had been bothering her, the feeling nagging at the back of her mind since she'd gotten the email from Bespoke had finally sunk in. It was fear.

What if she didn't win?

Finger Knitting

Materials:
Yarn
Fingers
(Scissors are helpful too!)

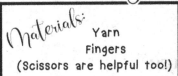

Start
Lace the yarn between your fingers. Tie a loose knot.

tie a knot

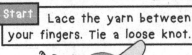

Lay yarn over your fingers above the lacing

Sequence

Fold
(your finger over)

Tuck
(your finger under the yarn)

Pull
(the yarn over your knuckle)

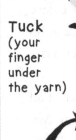

Loop
Repeat on all fingers

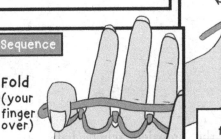

Selection
Check it out. Are you done?

If YES,
Then STOP
and tie off each finger loop

If NO
Then REPEAT
the other direction

17

DOWN A NOTCH

*A*mber navigated the crowded school halls on Monday, lost in thought. Design ideas churned around in her head. Something with Wren's yarn. Something else with Ivy's lights sewn into it. Kammie's necklace was beautiful and even Trixie was getting somewhere on the silly finger knitting. At least it seemed to keep her busy.

Her brain just couldn't concentrate on classes anymore. She'd even zoned out during science. Wren, of all people, had to elbow her to pay attention when Mr. Malcolm asked her a question. But it was hard when ideas for her collection scrambled relentlessly through her brain from the moment she woke up. She was even dreaming about ideas. There was so much to do! And it wasn't easy narrowing them down. There were so many possibilities.

Usually all it took to throw together a great outfit was a look in her closet, or shopping trip for inspiration. When designing something to sew, she mixed pictures of outfits online or from magazines or catalogs, things other people were wearing, and her own imagination with pattern pieces from her collection. This sleeve with that top, or add that bow to the top from this dress pattern and make it a shirt. But could her made-up designs compete with what high school kids invented?

Still, they were off to a good start. Sometimes the best ideas and the best outfits started with figuring out how to pull different pieces together, and everyone was making progress. They should have a bunch of elements ready by next weekend. She just had to figure out how to make it all work together.

Suddenly, a perky ponytail appeared in front of her. Amber almost crashed into it. She blinked and looked around, trying to orient herself. She was right next to Axel's locker. The blond girl, pulling out her lunchbox, had accidentally backed into her path. Now Amber had to say something or it would be weird.

"Hi," Amber smiled awkwardly. "Um. How's it going?"

"You almost ran into me." Axel put her hand on her hip.

"Sorry, I was thinking about something," Amber fidgeted. "Oh hey! Did I see you at Bespoke the other weekend? Did you end up applying for the internship after all?"

It was Axel's turn to fidget. She turned to close her locker, quickly hiding her suddenly trembling lips. When she turned around again, Axel's smile was back. Maybe Amber had imagined the sad expression.

"Yup. I figured if you were going to apply, I should too." Axel lifted her head and looked Amber in the eyes with a kind, sympathetic smile. "What a waste of time, huh?"

"Waste of time?" Amber couldn't bring herself to ask why Milo had been there too. Maybe it hadn't even been Milo.

"Well, yeah. I mean, I didn't see you, so I don't know if you were there, but there were all these rich high schoolers stuffing the box. You wouldn't believe it. They were so stylish it was painful." Axel began to head down to the lunch yard. Amber walked along with her, falling into old habits. "Kids like us never stood a chance. You know they already announced the finalists, right?"

It was almost like when they used to be friends. Walking and chatting together, headed to lunch. But once they got downstairs, Amber would go eat with her other friends. She wasn't even sure what Axel did for lunch anymore.

Come to think of it, she hadn't seen Milo around at lunch lately either. Maybe the two of them ate together. The thought stung. It wasn't any of her business, but Amber was surprised at her own tone when she replied.

"Actually, I do know," she told Axel. "Because I'm one of the finalists."

Axel stopped dead. Amber turned to look at her, raising her head and looking mercilessly at her former friend. What was she doing? But the icy feeling oozing off the memory of Axel and Milo walking away together seemed to control her body. Her mouth. It wasn't her business, she told herself again. Not any of her business at all. But as Axel stared in shock at her, Amber was surprised at how good it felt to be stared at with jealousy. It shouldn't, but it did.

"You..." Axel blinked. "You what?"

"I. Am. A. Finalist. I'm in the Fashion Face-Off," Amber sneered.

Axel didn't move. "That doesn't even make sense."

Amber frowned. "Why? Why doesn't it make sense, Axel? Do you think you're so much better than me? That people like you so much better? You're not, and they don't. I guess YOU didn't get in."

Amber flipped her gorgeous hair towards Axel as she turned to saunter off. But Axel's voice behind her made her foot freeze in mid-air.

"What's happened to you, Amber?" Axel's voice trembled. Amber wondered if she was starting to cry but didn't turn around to see. Axel kept talking to her back. "You used to be so nice. Now you're acting like some kind of spoiled brat. Why are you being mean?"

Amber set her foot down but didn't walk away or turn to face her. She spoke facing forward, hoping Axel could hear her above the noisy hall. "I'm not spoiled. I'm just stylish. You didn't believe in me, but you were wrong. And I'm going to win, too. You wait and see."

Neither one of them moved. Amber took a deep, shaky breath. Why did it feel so good to say that? It wasn't nice. It wasn't even true. Now if she didn't win, what would Axel say? Would she and Milo laugh about her? Together?

"Whatever." Axel pushed passed without even a glance, heading towards the cafeteria. "You always get all the attention. It's not even fair. Someone should take you down a notch."

18
———

CIRCUIT SEWING

*T*he bulb didn't light up.

Ivy and Amber sat in Amber's bedroom, trying to make a sewn circuit. It wasn't going as well as they'd imagined. Yet.

The theory was simple. Thread two embroidery needles with conductive thread. Put an LED on one end of a piece of fabric and a button battery on the other end. Then, stitch from the battery to the LED with one needle, and from the other side of the LED back to the battery with the other, making sure the stitch lines didn't touch each other. The conductive thread would create a path for the electricity to go from the battery, to the light, and back to the battery again in a circle. The LED would light up when the circuit was complete.

But in reality, it wasn't that easy.

They had bent the legs of the LED out on opposite sides, like it was doing the splits. But they kept sliding out from under the thread Amber sewed around each leg. So Ivy gently bent the wires into little loops while Amber carefully backed the stitches out of the fabric. Then she sewed it back down.

At first, the light lit up, but as they picked up the fabric, it flickered. Ivy looked closer.

"It's not tight enough yet," Ivy said. The comment reminded Amber about Mrs. Mailloux's idea to put "yet" after a problem.

Maybe it wasn't so stupid after all. Not tight enough yet. But this time it would be. She pulled the thread out once again and re-sewed it tighter around the leads, making sure the stitches were secure. Ivy pressed one needle to each side of the battery with one hand.

The bulb lit up.

"YES!" Ivy pumped her other fist in the air. "See? We figured it out."

"So the electricity goes down the conductive thread, then touches the metal of the sewing needles, right?" Amber ran through it again in her head. "That's why the light works?"

"Yup." Ivy continued to hold the metal needles against the battery as she inspected the rest of the circuit. "Metal is conductive. It's really easy for electricity to move through. And electricity likes to move through the easiest thing. Pretend there's a runner sitting inside the battery. She really wants to run. When metal touches the battery, it's like opening a door. The runner takes off. And since there are other runners behind her that want to run too, she can only go one way down the track."

"What makes the thread conductive?" Amber asked.

"I dunno," Ivy shrugged, looking closely at the stitching and the light. "Maybe it has tiny bits of metal in it? Like wire but more flexible? They usually wrap wire in an insulator, something it DOESN'T like running through, like rubber, so the electricity stays in the metal. But this thread isn't insulated, so we have to keep it from touching."

As Ivy tilted the fabric to see the underside of the circuit, the light flickered. She looked closely at the tails of thread dangling below the knots sewn into each thread. The tails were long, and as Ivy moved the fabric, they flopped against each other.

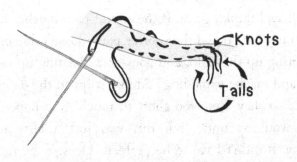

"Aha! Here's the short," Ivy pointed to the loose thread.

"Short?" Amber asked. "I made them long so the knots wouldn't pull out. If the tail is too short, the thread will slip back out through the knot, and it unties. You have to leave some thread at the end."

"No, look here," Ivy pushed the threads apart. The light lit up. Then she pushed them together and the light went dark.

"Whoa!" Amber reached out to try it. "Why does it do that?"

"It's called a short. The runner doesn't care what track she's going down, she's just running as fast as she can. If another path branches off the one she's supposed to be running along, she'll take it. So when these threads touch, it makes a new path that doesn't go to the light anymore. She just keeps running around not actually doing anything. It'll make the battery really hot. It might burn out or even spark. Electricity can be really dangerous. You have to show it respect because people are conductive too. We have little bits of electricity controlling things inside us, like our hearts."

"Okay, I think I get it. If the circuit path touches itself, the runner goes down the shorter path, doesn't do her job of lighting up the bulb, and goes crazy heating up everything and maybe exploding." Amber snipped the dangling strands so they were too short to touch. She hoped the knots wouldn't untie, but this was just a test circuit anyway. It didn't have to be perfect. "Doesn't the runner get tired and stop before exploding, though?"

"I mean, it's just an analogy," Ivy laughed. "Electricity is actually a complicated process I don't understand yet, but I always picture it like really fast race runners. A lot of people compare it to water flowing through pipes, but that confuses me because you are supposed to keep electricity away from water. Everybody connects to different things. Whatever it takes to help you understand."

Amber watched the light go on and off as she held the metal needles against the battery. She imagined a skirt with lights along the entire hem, drifting around her legs as she spun in a field of flowers at twilight.

"Looks like fairies," she whispered dreamily. Ivy looked at her quizzically and she explained. "I'm imagining a skirt lit up by LEDs, swishing around in the dark."

"Ah," Ivy nodded. "You know, I explained electricity to Trixie once using fast flying fairies instead of runners. Her dad got mad. He said it was silly and girly, but I don't know. It really connected with her."

"It's so sad how people think stuff girls like is automatically dumber than stuff that's not girly," Amber agreed. "That teaching something with trucks makes sense and is somehow more valid than teaching the same things with unicorns."

"Yeah. I'm starting to learn that. It's not okay." Ivy put an apologetic hand on Amber's arm. "I'm working on it. Though I never got that into fairies."

"Well, Trixie loves them, so your explanation made sense to her," Amber pointed out. "I don't think it's silly at all. She probably wouldn't have paid attention if you used water or trucks. That's just her, but I don't see why what she likes is any less valid than what anyone else likes. Anyway, we're lucky to have you to explain these things to us at all. You know so much about electronic stuff."

"Mom's been teaching me since I was tiny. She really wants me to understand it since she's an electrical engineer, I guess. But this is all pretty basic stuff."

"Not for me!" Amber laughed.

"Not yet," Ivy pointed out.

Amber tested the battery between the needles again. "You do the yet thing, huh?"

"The what?" Ivy asked absently.

"You know, put 'yet' at the end of a problem. It's supposed to be inspiring or something."

"I guess," Ivy mused. "I never really thought about it. Now, how do we attach the battery to the fabric so the thread stays connected to the correct sides and doesn't short it out?"

"Why don't we just sew it in place?" Amber asked.

"Because then the thread would touch both sides of the battery," Ivy explained. "One thread has to touch one side, the other has to touch the other side."

"What about the edges of the battery? Which side are they on?" Amber looked closely at the battery. The top seemed to fold over onto the sides. On the back of the battery there was a thin black ring separating the side edge from the back.

"The sides and top are positive. See the little plus sign? The bottom is negative." Ivy pointed out the thin black ring. "This black part keeps the two sides from touching. One of our conductive threads is sewn to the negative lead of the light, and the other is sewn to the positive one. That's called polarity, when you have a positive and negative side. You can't mix up the polarity. You have to hook up the correct lead to the correct battery side or it won't work."

"How do you know which lead of the LED light is positive and which is negative?" Amber asked.

"The negative is shorter." Ivy frowned at the LED leads, which were bent and already sewn down. "But since we can't tell which of these is the short one, we'll just have to test it first. If the light doesn't light up, we've attached the wrong sides. Then we'll just have to switch the threads to the other sides of the battery. It's not a big deal but we want to know which thread is which before we attach them, and I don't know how we're going to do that. Yet."

They smiled at each other. It actually did make Amber look at the problem differently.

"Usually you'd use a battery holder," Ivy pointed to the circuit. "But we don't have any, and don't have time to order one."

"Hmmm. Metal is conductive, right? So we can use something made of metal." Amber looked around her room.

Bits of paper, some rubber bands, a few paper clips, decorative erasers, and a pen cluttered the top of her desk. Wait. Paper clips are metal.

"What do you think?" Amber held one up. "I could sew the thread around the curved ends."

"Yeah." Ivy looked at it closely. "Yeah, I think we can work with that. Paper clips are big enough to make a good connection to the battery. We'd need two, one for the positive and one for the negative sides."

Ivy dug in her backpack and pulled out an almost empty roll of black, stretchy tape. Putting one paper clip on each side of the button battery, she tightly wrapped the tape around the paper clip-and-battery sandwich. The tape stretched, pulling the paper clips super tight against the battery.

"What's that?" Amber asked, fascinated.

"Electrical tape!" Ivy replied as she finished wrapping her bundle. "It sticks, insulates, and stretches to make a tight connection all at once."

Amber took the completed bundle. When one needle touched each paper clip, the light lit up.

She sewed each paper clip to the fabric with the correct needle, completing the circuit.

"Look at that!" she exclaimed. "We figured it out!"

Suddenly, Ivy's cell phone began to sing. She scrambled to dig it out of the bottom of her backpack.

As Ivy brought the phone to her ear, Amber could hear shouting from the other end.

"Wait, wait," Ivy called into the phone. "Just hang on, Wren, I'm putting you on speaker."

She clicked the screen and a frantic squeal filled the room. It was Wren.

"You guys! You have to come immediately. RIGHT NOW! Everything's destroyed!"

Sewn Circuit (part 1)

Materials: Conductive thread
Coin Cell (Button) Battery
2 large-eyed embroidery needles
Electrical tape
Strip of fabric
1 LED

Place a paperclip on each side of the battery, and wrap tightly with electrical tape.

Cut 2 lengths of conductive thread, about 20 inches long each. Thread them into two embroidery needles and knot the ends of each.

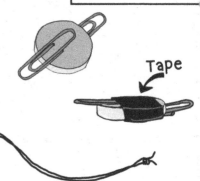

Tape

Sewing Tip:

Secure your thread by passing the needle through the two threads near the knot and pulling it tight.

Tightly stitch each paperclip to one end of the fabric with a different needle.

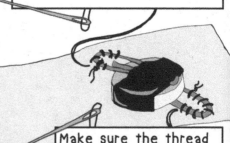

Make sure the thread doesn't touch the side of the battery.

Sewing Tip:

Running Stitch - running the needle up and down through fabric without backstitching.

Bend the legs of the LED so they loop and lay flat.

Use a Running Stitch to sew from the battery to the other side of the fabric strip with each separate needle. Make sure to sew the paths away from each other so the threads don't touch.

Test the POLARITY (the positive and negative sides) by touching one needle to each side of the LED. If the light doesn't turn on, flip the LED around and try again. When you find the right sides, sew each side down with the correct needle.

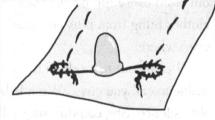

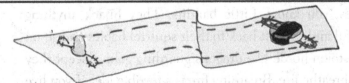

Without a switch to turn the light off, your sewn circuit will keep glowing until the battery runs out! You can replace the battery by unwrapping the tape. Can you figure out a way to turn it off and on?

19

IT GETS COMPLICATED

The Greenhouse looked like a crime scene. The easel lay on its side next to an overturned stool. Supplies were strewn all over the tables and floor, dumped out from every bin on the lower shelves. Amber's leftover clothes hung from bins and stools, and puddled in clumps everywhere.

"I came out to work on the yarn and saw this. So I ran inside to call you guys," Wren babbled into the uncomfortable silence. She couldn't stop talking. "It's gotta be squirrels. There are squirrels all over. Squirrels are terrible thieves, you know. Little bandits. They hijack anything colorful and carry it back to their squirrel babies and sit on their stolen horde like dragons guarding gold. Except they don't breathe fire. Breathing fire is a terrible idea if you live in a tree. Do you think they're still here?"

"Who was the last one to leave Sunday?" Amber groaned. "Did we close the door tightly?"

No one answered. The door was open now.

Ivy crept cautiously inside, kicking away an overturned stool. She grabbed a long yardstick and poked at a pile of fabric, half expecting a squirrel or rat to jump out. Nothing did. Ivy poked at another pile. Nothing came out of that one either.

Then one of the bins that overturned on the floor seemed to move slightly. They could see it rock, just a little bit. The movement was almost too small to see.

"Look out," she whispered, edging around it with her yardstick. "Hold the door open but don't block it."

Amber pushed herself deeper into the balding wisteria and held the door open from behind. Kammie and Wren scampered away, moving around to peer through the windows as Ivy approached the bin.

"Did it just wiggle?" Wren asked Kammie, who didn't answer. "I thought I saw it wiggle. If there's a squirrel in there, look out because squirrels can bite when they're angry. Like my sister. But it probably hurts worse when a squirrel bites you. And my mom wouldn't be able to yell at it like she would yell at Trixie. But Trix doesn't really bite that much any-"

"Shut up, Wren," Kammie whispered, waving at her to be quiet.

Ivy got in position and reached out the yardstick, flipping the bin over in one smooth motion.

Something brown and large flipped into the air, flapping wildly.

All four of them screamed, but the brown thing drifted

harmlessly to the floor. It was just one of Amber's old shirts that had been underneath the bin. Ivy must have tossed it up with the tip of the yardstick as she flipped the bin. Then she saw the bin had been wobbling over a pair of scissors. The wind from the open door must have moved it a little. The Greenhouse was officially clear of rodents.

But it was not clear of mess. A very angry squirrel must have had a massive squirrel tantrum to result in this kind of destruction.

Kammie gasped all of a sudden and pushed past everyone, running towards the table where she'd left her beaded necklace. The strand, snapped in two, sagged over the table. Beads scattered all over the floor. Apparently, a squirrel had not secreted them away to a hidden treasure trove. A trail of beads led out the door. Through the windows, she caught a glimpse of red near the edge of the yard outside.

"What else is missing?" Kammie cried, counting the beads she could find. Almost half of them were gone.

Amber, feeling numb, edged inside. Wren sank onto a stool, picking up some tangled yarn from the floor. She threw it on top of the table angrily.

In a pattering of footsteps, Trixie appeared in the doorway. Her knitting dangled from the back of one hand and the other clenched a ball of yarn. She took one look inside at them, screamed, and ran back into the house.

"Right? Me too!" Amber called, burying her face in her hands. "Me too."

20

MORAL FIBER

"What are we gonna do?" Kammie cradled her remaining beads protectively, refusing to put them in the plastic container Ivy offered.

"I don't even know." Amber sat on the floor, shoveling clothes back into a bag.

"We're obviously going to start again." Ivy put her hands on her hips. "Come on, it's not that bad. Nothing looks broken."

Kammie held up the handful of beads and their broken string.

"Sorry," Ivy cringed. "I mean, not much is broken. We can't let a little setback stop us! We have to persist!"

"Hey Ivy, can we please not make everything into a learning experience?" Wren draped herself dramatically over the potting table. "This sucks."

Ivy turned away with a frown.

Wren plopped her hand over her face and moaned.

"We have to do something," Ivy mumbled. "Doing nothing never accomplishes anything."

"Well," Amber sighed, "I guess we can start by cleaning up, right? I mean, what else can we do?"

"I was all ready to make yarn." Wren rolled off the table, landing on her feet like a cat, and gathered cardboard scraps from the floor.

"You can still make yarn. Please do," Amber nodded. "But it's a school night. Mom wants me home. Let's just take a few minutes to pick up this stuff so you can work tomorrow after school, okay? At least it'll be a little forward movement."

"The next right step," Kammie whispered sadly. "Just take the next right step, no matter how small, right?"

Amber nodded.

"That's what I said," Ivy grumbled.

"Okay, well," said Wren, "the yarn is made from old t-shirts, so maybe I can start cleaning those up. That way I can look for ones I can use."

Wren gathered clothes from the floor, hanging from the shelves, and cluttering the tables. She extracted shirts that didn't have printed designs on them, didn't have any side seams, and were nice colors. She shoved everything else back into the laundry bags.

"I don't know where to start," wailed Kammie, clutching her beads.

"Just grab the nearest thing and put it away," Ivy said. "Just start with one thing. Then do the next. Then keep going until we're done. There's nothing else we can do."

ALONE IN THE Greenhouse after school the next day, Wren smoothed out a blue shirt. YouTube said t-shirt yarn was thick and strong and that she'd only need a shirt, a yardstick or ruler, some sharp scissors, a marker, and permission to destroy the shirt.

Yesterday, Amber had given her that permission. Sort of. She'd asked if she could use the shirts she'd picked out and Amber had shrugged and sorted more cardboard. Obviously that meant yes.

The sharpest, strongest scissors were in an untouched bin on the top shelf which had probably been too high for the squirrels to get at. Or maybe they'd worked out their squirrely anger on the lower shelves. Either way, the scissors were undamaged. Wren clambered up to grab the bin.

The videos recommended using a rolling cutter and cutting mat, but they didn't have one. She considered using a pizza cutter, which looked the same, but it probably wasn't sharp enough. She'd just have to make do with scissors.

Turning back to the shirt that lay flat on the table, she smoothed it one more time. Then, keeping it as flat as possible, she slid the scissors under the fabric at one armpit and cut across to the other, snipping off the whole top of the shirt. Then she cut off the hem, the bottom part where the fabric was folded over. That left a tube of fabric without any seams or stitching.

She smoothed out the tube again. Evidently it was

important to keep it really flat, so the cuts were as straight as possible. Then she used the yardstick Ivy had gone squirrel hunting with to measure along the top fold of the tube from raw edge to raw edge, marking a little dot every inch. Moving the yardstick to the bottom, she used the marker to dot every inch there too, so they lined up.

Basically, she was going to cut from dot to dot across the tube from the bottom fold, but stop about an inch from the top fold. She'd watched a lot of videos and they all were a little different, but every one said how important it was NOT to cut all the way through the top of the tube. When she was done, she was supposed to have kind of a fringe, like a fabric comb or something. If she cut through that, she'd just get a bunch of strips of fabric, not a long piece of yarn.

"Shoot!" Wren mumbled to herself. "It would have been easier if I'd put the yardstick on top of the fabric and marked the dots underneath it. That way I could just stop at the dots!"

She shrugged and laid the yardstick from a bottom to a top dot. Sliding her scissors under the fabric tube, she followed along its edge to cut up to the upper dot, but remembered to stop before she cut through the top.

It was hard to remember every time, but again, and again, and again she cut up through the folded fabric without cutting the inch strip on top. After the first few cuts, she abandoned the yardstick entirely, and just eyeballed her cuts, trying to keep the strip width as even as she could.

What an accomplishment! she thought as she finished up, massaging the back of her neck.

The next step was the tricky part. The place where the magic happened. The final cuts went diagonally across the part she hadn't cut, the top of the fabric comb. It involved concentration. Not exactly Wren's favorite thing.

She had to cut from one strip to the next. Like when you buttoned one wrong button on a sweater and messed up the entire row. Everything was off one. But to do that, she had to open up the tube, so what used to be the top edge was really in the middle, with fringy teeth going off each end, like ribs sticking out from a chest bone.

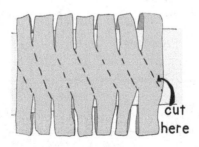

cut
here

Shaking out the fabric, she slid the tube onto her arm so she wouldn't accidentally cut anything but the small strip of fabric between the ribs. Taking a deep breath, she carefully opened the scissors and put one side under the fabric. She felt them slide over her skin as she got them in place.

Then, with a quick snip, she'd made the first cut!

After that it was surprisingly easy. Using that cut as a guide, she lined up the next one. Snip, snip, snip. Before she knew it, she'd gotten to the end! One quick diagonal snip and the whole thing opened up into one long strip.

Through some mathematical magic she didn't quite understand, the wide tube had become one long thin strip! Running it through her hands, she tugged the whole strip gently, bit by bit, until it curled onto itself. And just like that, it became thick, strong, colorful, awesome yarn.

It looked great! Totally unique thick, chunky yarn! And, as she wrapped it into a ball, she realized just how much yarn there was to work with. She'd let Amber figure out what to do with it.

Wren tossed her yarn ball into the air and caught it. She couldn't wait to show Amber at school tomorrow.

T-Shirt Yarn

Materials:

Marker
Yardstick or ruler
Sharp scissors or a rolling cutter and mat
Old t-shirts (with no side seams) & permission to destroy them

Cut the top and hem off the shirt

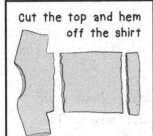

Smooth the shirt flat.
Mark 1-1.5 inches along the top and bottom with a dot.

← cut line

Cut between the dots, stopping about an inch from the top so the strips hang in a row.

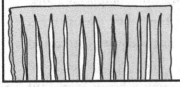

Open the tube and snip from one strip to the next in a diagonal.
Tug on the long strip until the sides roll up.

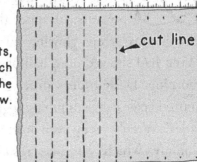

cut here

BAM, you're done! Yarn!

21

RECOVERY ATTEMPT

*B*y Thursday, Amber felt better about their progress, despite the squirrel attack. The circuit was safely glowing away in her bedroom, and Wren had showed off a ball of awesome t-shirt yarn that morning. Design ideas drifting around in her head had started coalescing, clumping together like bioplastic molecules. Wren's mom even loaned them her dressmaker's dummy, which was like a soft mannequin you could adjust to any size you wanted. They could use it to assemble the outfits. Some of Kammie's beads were still missing, but she'd put on a brave face and said it didn't matter. Amber suspected it really, really did, but since she didn't know how to make Kammie feel better, Amber just sort of ignored it and hoped it would get better with a little time.

Swooshing into Social Studies, chatting happily with Ivy, Amber felt once again like she really could win. Ivy and Amber sat at their desks on the opposite sides of the classroom just as the bell rang.

Today, Amber wore the turquoise dress with a handkerchief hem that she'd made herself, paired with a pure white cardigan and sparkling garnet earrings. Her long hair sat artfully arranged in a messy bun. She flashed Mrs. Mailloux a brilliant smile. Noticing Amber's rejuvenated perkiness, the teacher smiled back with a little nod of satisfaction.

"So, class," she began, and this time Amber paid as much attention to her words as the French accent. "Today is the day we begin the project we've been talking about."

Amber's smile began to fade.

What project? Now?

The Renegades were just hitting their stride! They were on a roll! They'd triumphed over the squirrel obstacle and now it was supposed to be smooth sailing. Happily ever after. The movie montage of everyone working together before the triumphant and unexpected win! Obstacles weren't supposed to keep coming at this point.

Desperately replaying the last few weeks in her mind, Amber couldn't remember hearing anything about any project. Wait, no. She did vaguely remember the other kids taking some notes. She should have paid better attention.

It would be okay. Maybe it wouldn't be a big project.

"It will be a big project," Mrs. Mailloux continued. "Worth a good part of your grade, so as we discussed last week, make sure you have the time to work on it."

A wave of nausea hit Amber full on. She glanced at Ivy

from across the room. Ivy listened to the teacher attentively, her notebook out and ready.

Right. Amber should be taking notes. Pay attention now, worry about time management later. Ivy knew how to balance a lot of commitments. She'd have some pointers.

"Your presentations will be in three weeks," Mrs. Mailloux walked through the aisles handing out sheets of paper. Amber scrambled to copy down the information in her notebook. "Choose the industry you will focus on. You will have some class time, so try to get as much done as possible. Now, we will continue to discuss globalization to help you get started. Please open your notebooks."

The other kids were just now pulling out their notebooks and pencils. Apparently this project was only news to Amber. Apparently everyone else paid actual attention in sixth grade. Oh no.

Mrs. Mailloux set a paper on top of Amber's notebook. It explained the assignment: research a worldwide major industry using at least two sources, then write a three- to five-page paper to present to the class. OMG. Three to five PAGES? Of her own research? AND present it? That was a lot more work than she was used to. This was a serious project. Amber was used to putting in a little effort and getting pretty decent grades. This was a whole other level. It would seriously eat into her fashion time!

And what about Ivy? She was already maxed out. Would she still be able to help between her sports commitments and this stupid report?

Amber took off her cardigan, feeling sweaty. Well,

okay. She would just have to pick something easy. Could she combine the research with her fashion designs somehow? Groaning, Amber sank into her chair, unable to focus on Mrs. Mailloux. Fear crept up her belly.

Just take notes, she told herself. *You can figure everything out later.*

Her pencil was under her cardigan. As she lifted the sweater, she read *Made in Bangladesh* on its label. Inspiration rushed in like a knight in shining armor. She'd research the global fashion industry!

Maybe the report could even HELP her designs with some global inspiration. There were amazing fashion trends all across the globe. Japan's designs were particularly stunning.

That was it, then. Solved! She breathed a sigh of relief and promised herself she wouldn't get caught unaware again. Reinvigorated, Amber bent to her notes, listening attentively to everything Mrs. Mailloux said.

22

RABBIT HOLE

"*A*lright, Google, talk to me," Amber told the laptop. She sat in her quiet room, the door closed and locked, with a steaming mug of tea next to her. Cozy and determined. Removing her rings and bracelets, she laid her hands lightly on the keyboard. "Let's get this over with."

It was a research paper, so she'd have to research. And there was no better research than a web search. But what should she search for? With all of human knowledge at her fingertips, she had to be pretty specific about her search terms, or she'd end up watching videos of hamsters in tiny costumes all night long.

Amber typed in *Fashion Industry Around The World*.

Over four million results appeared immediately. Flashes of fabulous runway outfits from Milan, Paris, and New York caught her attention, but she forced herself not to get sucked down an endless rabbit hole of links. Runway fashion was not what she was looking for right now, not the kind of global industry focus she was supposed to be researching.

So what was she really researching? Or, as the Engineering Design Process said: what's the problem? She had to identify her question before she could answer it.

The problem was that she had to write a ridiculously long paper when she was supposed to be working on her designs. But that wasn't a problem Google could solve. Google wasn't a solution, it was a tool. It couldn't tell you what to ask, or which answer was the right one. It wouldn't think for you, it could only answer your questions. And if you didn't use it properly, you could waste a lot of time.

And she didn't have a lot of time.

She sipped her tea.

Actually, the problem was that she needed to find information about the global fashion industry in a way that would give her a little inspiration, too. A way to make four million websites into a three- to five-page paper. Four million websites was a lot of information. Most of it probably wouldn't even work for her report. She needed better search terms.

She needed to narrow it down.

The more specific she got, the more accurate her information would be. Maybe she needed to add a word like *global*. Global AND fashion AND industry AND world. AND would give her much better results then OR.

Okay, adding *global*.

"Global, global, global," she mumbled, scrolling through

the hits. The words *Supply Chain* caught her eye. Hmmm. There was something about supply chains in her notes. She dug out her notebook and flipped through the pages. Apparently, supply chains were "a system of people and activities that move a product from raw materials, through production, then distribution, all the way to the end user."

Well, that certainly sounded global. She thought about the Bangladesh label in her cardigan. Since Bangladesh was in another part of the world, that made it global. What part of the supply chain was Bangladesh? She guessed it was probably production.

Turning to a new page in her notebook, she wrote *Fun Facts About the Fashion Industry* and jotted down a few notes. After another small sip of her tea, Amber stretched and laid her hands back on the keyboard.

She skimmed the headlines of her search results for information on supply chains or even just Bangladesh. Where was Bangladesh anyway? She didn't even know what continent it was on. A little embarrassing, considering how many of her clothes came from there, but she'd find it on a map later.

She scrolled past headlines that read *How To Get Started In The Fashion Industry, Most Popular Design Shows Around The World*, and *Which Country's Style Are You? Take This Quiz To Find Out*. None of them looked right. Finally, she found a promising one.

Statistics Of The Global Fashion Industry.

Mrs. Mailloux loved statistics. Statistics might not be fun facts, but they'd get her a good grade. The website turned out to be pretty boring though, so she bookmarked it to come back to when she figured out exactly what she needed.

She also bookmarked the quiz to come back to later and tried not to wonder which country's style she was. She refocused on the screen.

Multiple sources meant more research, so she opened a new browser tab and re-typed her query in the top bar as *Statistics Of The Global Fashion Industry*.

Feeling a little guilty, she scrolled past the boring sounding *Statistics and Numbers of the Global Apparel Market*, and instead clicked on the much more exciting 30 *Shocking Facts and Figures About the Global Apparel and Textile Industry*. A list appeared, with paragraphs of facts nicely contained and numbered with giant, brightly colored numerals.

"Right," Amber picked up her purple pen and started taking notes. "Now we're getting somewhere. The global textile and garment industry is worth nearly...Wait, that can't be right. 3,000 TRILLION DOLLARS!? Three thousand trillion dollars? That IS shocking! Is that even a number?"

She shook her head and leaned back, trying to conceptualize it. Where exactly did those numbers come from? What did they mean? Another quick search told her there were fewer than eight billion people on Earth. How many dollars each was that? No, that must be wrong. She didn't even know there was that much money on Earth. She opened yet another browser just to verify. That one said THREE trillion dollars. Must have been a typo. Three thousand BILLION dollars was the same as three trillion. Or maybe they were talking about over the lifetime of the fashion industry. Either way, even three trillion dollars was an unbelievable amount of money.

She turned back to the next shocking fact and blurted, "People in Manhattan spend HOW MUCH on clothing a MONTH? Well, that might have something to do with the three trillion dollars! Every single month? Everyone? Even the babies and little kids and people who don't care about wearing clothes, and people who don't have a lot of money? The fashion people must spend a LOT to make up for the ones that don't spend much at all. Where would they even put all those clothes?"

Her Aunt Molly and Uncle Tim lived in Manhattan, and their apartment was tiny. How much did they spend on clothes? Amber glanced over at her own full closet. Even after getting rid of all those bags, it was packed. So was her dresser. Its bottom drawer overflowed with pajama pants. Her shoes mounded in the bottom of the closet, including ones she'd never even worn.

She thought back to her first conversation with Jewels.

What do I do with this stuff, she'd asked.

That's the question, Jewels had replied.

Where does it all go when I'm done with it? It couldn't ALL go in bags in the Greenhouse. Did everyone in Manhattan have their own laundry bags full of old clothes? Did they add new bags every year? Multiply that by the number of people in Manhattan. She didn't know how many people lived there exactly, but it had to be *lots*.

On a whim, she opened another tab and typed "How many trees are on earth."

Scanning the taglines that came up, she estimated about three trillion.

"Wait," she said to herself. "That's like a dollar of fashion industry to every single tree in the world. That's weird. That just can't be right."

She wrote it down in her notebook under Fun Facts even though the fact wasn't really all that fun. It was kind of upsetting, honestly. Could she make it more fun for her report? What if she replaced the search terms with Tree Fashion?

Who doesn't love trees? She thought.

Immediately, images of dresses made from bark and leaves rewarded her. That was fun! One model wore white branches strapped over a black bodysuit, and another had branches sticking out of her hair. A fluffy puff of long green fur looked like a coat made of leaves, with actual leaves sticking out of it at all sorts of angles.

And there were a surprisingly large number of dresses that looked like Christmas trees. Their full skirts seemed to be made out of pine branches wrapped over hoop skirts, with little red ornaments strewn around. Amber snorted.

At least be original, she thought, as image after image of basically the same dress scrolled past. Rolling her eyes, she clicked back to her original search and started scrolling again.

A few links down from the top, she stopped at *The Fashion Industry and its Carbon Footprint.*

She clicked it.

The website iloveheplanet.com loaded, fresh and stylish in white and spring green, with pictures of trees and a logo of a bird surrounded by leaves. Deciduous leaves, Amber thought automatically. Looked like birch or cotton-wood. She started to read.

And froze.

Her heart began to pound faster.

As she stared at the first line in the article, the room around her went blurry. She began to feel dizzy.

"The fashion industry is one of the most polluting industries in the world, second only to the gas and oil industry."

One of the most polluting industries in the world.

Second to oil and gas.

Amber's hands dropped off the keyboard. She leaned back heavily. Reached a trembling hand toward her slowly cooling mug to take another sip of tea, she blinked a few times. Maybe she just wasn't reading it correctly. She shook her head, then looked again.

But the text didn't change.

23

WORSE THAN GRASS-NADOS?

"*O*IL AND GAS!" Amber yelled.

Kammie cringed. Wren looked up sharply. The Renegades had met early on Saturday, as planned, because that afternoon was Amber's salon appointment with her mom. But instead of getting work done, they were watching Amber melt down. And it got worse the more she told them about what she'd discovered.

Amber closed her eyes and took some deep breaths. "Oil. And gas. Gas, people. My clothes have tree blood on them."

"Isn't tree blood sap?" Wren asked. "I've gotten that on my clothes before, too. It's really hard to get off."

"Tree blood." Amber glared at her. "The blood of trees. Dead trees. But sticky. Like oil, not sap. Poisonous, seagull-killing, pipeline-leaking oil. Only worse, because unlike oil, my clothes smell good and look fabulous!"

She kicked one of the laundry bags. It felt good, so she

kicked it a few more times. Then she growled angrily and kicked it again. The bag fell over. Amber screamed at it, releasing some of her frustration, and kicked it back into place.

Trixie hadn't come into the Greenhouse since the first squirrel attack, but she was out in the yard refilling her bird feeder when Amber screamed. Dropping her bag of sunflower seeds, she poked her head in the door.

"Are you okay?"

"Oil and gas, Trixie!" Amber pleaded with her, as if the six-year-old could fix things. "It's horrible!"

Trixie came inside, her finger-knit chain still dangling from the back of her hand, and threw her arms around Amber. Amber buried her face in the girl's tangled brown hair with a whimper.

"So..." Ivy answered calmly. "You got some work done on your report then?"

"I don't think you understand how serious this is," Amber shot back angrily. "I mean, really serious."

"Well," Ivy scratched her nose. "I don't think the fashion industry has changed since you started your research. I mean, how bad can it be? We've learned about oil and gas, plastics, and cars all polluting the environment. We've even learned about the impact of cow farts on climate change. But I, at least, haven't heard about FASHION as a culprit."

"Cow farts pollute the air?" Trixie started laughing. She laughed so hard she had to let go of Amber.

"Maybe it's because they smell so bad," Wren replied.

She wrote 'Danger Farts at Work' on a scrap of paper and drew a cow next to it. Then she drew a bunch of wiggly lines coming from the cow's backside. She couldn't stop giggling.

"Even worse than Daddy's farts?" Trixie doubled over with laughter.

Even Kammie started to chuckle.

"No, wait, wait, wait, maybe..." Trixie gasped for air. "Is it because...is it because they eat so much grass that they fart grass-nados?"

Amber threw up her hands. "There is no such thing as a GRASS-NADO, Trixie! This is serious! Fashion is ruining the planet!"

"So," Wren squinted at her, "we're not making fashion stuff today?"

"I don't know." Amber buried her face in her hands. "I don't know, I don't know! I can't handle all this."

"All what?" Ivy asked sternly. "Come on, we've got work to do."

"EVERYTHING!" Amber cried. "I've been so stupid because I didn't even know the harm I was causing to nature, which is what I'm supposed to be so smart about! Maybe I am just a dumb princess after all, not a scientist."

"Princesses aren't dumb," Trixie said. "And anyway, I thought you were both."

"I keep saying that." Amber shook her head. "But am I really? What kind of scientist doesn't even know the destruction they are causing? That's like being the worst kind of princess. The dumb, vain, selfish kind. This research changed everything. Now that I know about the waste and pollution of the fashion industry, I see it everywhere. I see what the whole fashion industry has done — what I'VE done. That's probably why the squirrels ripped apart all our stuff! We're destroying their homes!"

Trixie's eyes widened in fear and she ran out the door, her finger knitting flying out behind her like a tail. She didn't even stop to pick up the bag of seeds.

"That's right, Trixie," Amber called after her, "I wish I could run away from what I learned, too. It's terrifying what I've done to nature! I don't even blame the squirrels!"

"Well, we can take care of that problem at least. Dad got me a screw-in latch from the hardware store." Wren pointed to a large hook in a package on the table. "It's so weird, though! We've never had a problem with squirrels before."

"I told you," Amber griped. "They're mad. Mad because the fashion industry is destroying nature."

"How?" Kammie asked quietly. "How is it destroying nature?"

Amber took two deep breaths. The thoughts racing through her brain slowed down, and she could start to put them in order. Start to think more clearly.

"All sorts of ways," Amber finally replied. "I don't even remember them all, and I was up all night reading about it."

"Do we want to find out?" Wren offered, unsure. "I can go get the iPad."

"Knowledge is power," Ivy nodded.

Wren zipped into her house and returned with an iPad. She began poking at it before she even got back.

"I don't think I'm using the right search terms," she thrust the device at Amber. "I keep getting websites about water pollution. Clothes don't have anything to do with water."

"Actually, they do. From start to finish. It takes a lot of water to grow cotton, for one thing." Amber turned the screen to face them. "Look here, it takes six hundred and fifty GALLONS of water to make ONE t-shirt. That's like flushing the toilet four or five hundred times. For one shirt!"

The others stared at the website.

"Then dyeing the fabric is super awful and puts all these toxic chemicals into the water," Amber continued. "And it's really polluting because it's done in places where the government doesn't even try to stop it. There aren't any rules or anything. And then there are microfibers."

"Microfibers?" Wren asked.

Kammie picked up the iPad, reading it out loud. "Microfibers are tiny bits that come off clothes when we wash them. They get in the waste water that dumps out from the washing machine into the ocean."

"See?" Wren frowned. "It's good I don't put my clothes in the hamper."

"But isn't waste water processed? To catch stuff like that?" Kammie asked. "I mean, there aren't laundry suds in our drinking water, right? It goes through some kind of cleaning?"

"I have no idea, but they get to the ocean somehow and fish eat those little fibers. And most of our clothes are made of synthetic fibers. Man-made polymers. That means there's plastic in a lot of those fibers. And it isn't bioplastic," Amber added ominously. "Though I don't think bioplastic is any better as fish food."

"So, what?" Wren asked. "We're all supposed to go naked?"

"Don't be absurd." Ivy rolled her eyes. "Every industry pollutes. They also give people jobs to buy food and medicine, and everything. Businesses are the backbone of countries, like Mrs. Mailloux said. Think about how many people are employed by the fashion industry."

Kammie and Wren looked at each other, confused. Was the fashion industry good or bad?

Amber paused, too. It was true. From people cutting and sewing clothes, growing cotton, making synthetic fabric, weaving cloth, dyeing it, all the way through to the scientists inventing new fibers and special fabrics, the fashion industry gave jobs to thousands, maybe even millions of people. Even fashion designers, models, and Jewels selling stuff at the store. They all had jobs because of the clothes Amber bought. The whole supply chain. She wondered about how much the people in Bangladesh made for every cardigan she danced around in. She'd have to look that up later.

"I don't know," Amber said more quietly, staring at the iPad screen. "But what I kept reading again and again is that the main issue is waste. 85 percent of all textiles go into the dump each year. That means almost as many clothes are thrown away each year as are made. Every year. Where do they all go? They don't just disappear."

They all looked over at the bags in the corner. Amber knew that if she hadn't brought them to the consignment store, she probably would have tossed them in the garbage and never thought about them again. Or maybe donated them. How much clothing got donated to charity stores each year by people who wanted to do the right thing? People who then went right out and bought a bunch more cheap clothes to replace the ones they just donated. Clothes they didn't really need.

How many of those donated clothes got bought before the next wave of donations came in? What happened to everything that didn't get bought?

Amber needed to think. She handed the iPad to Kammie and stepped outside. Wren stood to go after her, but Ivy put a hand on her shoulder.

"I think she just needs some air," Ivy said gently, watching Amber through windows framed by the leafless wisteria as she stepped into a little patch of sunlight outside. But Wren pulled away and ran to Amber, joining her in the sunlight. Kammie looked at Ivy uncertainly, but Ivy just shook her head.

Out in the yard, Wren stood next to her best friend as they both gazed at the neighbor's giant tree towering over them.

"Do you want to make some stuff today?" Wren asked

gently. "Would that help you feel better? It always helps me."

"I don't know what I want," Amber shrugged. "I don't think I can do anything at all right now. You know, the internship was the most important thing ever to me. Something I could really be good at. Something I could win. I wanted people to see me, see what I'm capable of. I just want to be somebody special. Just yesterday it was all I could think about. And now? Now I can't even think about it at all."

"Well, you're my best friend," Wren said softly. "I think you're super special."

Amber didn't say anything. She looked away and wiped at her eyes with the back of her hand. Wren gently placed a hand on her arm.

"I feel like 'special' is this cat we're all chasing, you know?"

Amber looked up quizzically. Wren continued.

"Like, it's lying over on the other side of the room in a sunbeam and you just know its fur is silky and warm and you want to squish your face against it and snuggle in the sunbeam too, so you can get that cat-in-a-sunbeam feeling. You start petting it and it's just as warm and silky as you'd thought. Then it suddenly rolls over and claws your arm to shreds and dashes away and you're all like, 'What the heck just happened?!?' But you still want that sunbeam feeling cuz it was awesome. So you chase the cat and maybe you catch it, but you probably don't, because it's a cat, right? And have you ever tried to catch a cat that didn't want to be caught? But let's say you did. Catch it, I mean — let's say you caught it somehow. And you try to force it back in the sunbeam but it's like 'No way, sucker! I'm a cat! You can't make me!' and even if it doesn't shred you with its vicious claws again, it still won't go back to sleep in the sunbeam if you're trying to force it. You know?"

There was a long pause. Then Amber nodded. "I think I understand."

"Cats are wise, Amber. You should learn from them." Wren patted her on the arm and turned, heading back inside the Greenhouse, leaving Amber alone with her thoughts.

Picking up the sunflower seeds, Amber put a handful into Trixie's bird feeder and set the bag on the fence. The sunlight lit her hair up like fire. A light breeze swished her skirt softly around her legs as she hugged her jacket tightly around her shoulders. A fairytale princess all alone, lost in the woods.

Running her fingers through the lengths of her soft hair again and again, Amber didn't feel like a princess anymore, no matter what she wore.

Did she even want to? She felt like a snake shedding her skin. Like the trees and plants around her, like the wisteria losing and regrowing its leaves, like one season drifting into the next. She could feel herself changing. The only problem was that she had no idea where to go from here.

Yet.

24

ALREADY PLANNED

"We're leaving in half an hour, honey," Amber's mom called up to her.

Amber sat despondent on her bed that afternoon. Looking at stuff.

Stuff.

Stuff was everywhere. Soft and fluffy and velvety and pastel. So much stuff. Did she really need all this stuff? She looked down at her delicate dress, surrounding her legs like a cloud. It was absolutely gorgeous.

It didn't feel right.

On the desk, books waited patiently in her new backpack. Beyond the backpack, Amber saw all its plastic packaging still stuffed into the garbage can. There was more packaging than backpack. And it had come from Italy. Which meant it traveled from Italy. On some combination of planes, boats, and trucks. All the way across the world to sit in the corner, unused. Gathering dust. It had seemed so romantic back when she ordered it. Now all she could think of was how much pollution she'd caused for something she didn't even need.

She still loved the backpack, it just didn't seem romantic anymore. And her beautiful dress felt silly. She didn't know where it came from, originally.

She opened her closet and ran her hands across the flowing, sparkling garments. Why didn't they feel right anymore? She pulled down the expensive lilac dress she'd worn the day she tried to tell the others about the internship. It did look like a princess dress, all grown up and classy. A dress to be worn by someone smart, confident, fashionable — and naive. Innocent. Someone romantic inside.

Not all princesses were innocent, of course, and they certainly weren't stupid. Another person wearing these clothes might feel empowered by them. She used to. But now, these dresses felt like the innocent girl she was yesterday morning. A girl who believed in fairy tales. A princess who ignored her impact on the planet. Looking at them made her angry.

The lilac dress hurtled across the Amber's pink bedspread, followed by delicate, flowing dress after dress after dress.

"I'm NOT a princess anymore!" screamed Amber, throwing a tulle skirt toward the pile. It floated up and got caught in the delicate netting draped over her four-poster bed. "And I'm not STUPID! How could I be so STUPID?? STUPID STUPID!!!"

She marched away from her closet and yanked the skirt hard. The bed's gossamer netting *riiiipped*. She tugged the torn netting down from the frame completely. The bed shook.

She stomped to the door and threw the wad of fabric violently out into the hall. It fluttered gracefully to the floor.

With another scream, she slammed the door shut. Then, just for good measure, opened the door and slammed it again. Then she turned back to her room with vengeance in her eyes.

Footsteps ran toward her room from out in the hall as she yanked dresser drawers open and pulled out clouds of satin, sheers, and lacy pastels. The footsteps paused outside her door and, after a second, a gentle knock followed.

"Honey?" her mom's voice called in. "Are you alright? What's going on?"

Amber didn't answer. She sank into a heap on the floor, trying to melt into the shag of her rug. She covered her eyes with her hands and breathed. One, two. One, two.

It wasn't working.

The doorknob turned. The door opened quietly. Amber heard her mom gasp, then the click of high heels delicately stepping into the wreckage of her room. The sound disappeared as the heels crossed over her rug, coming toward her.

Hands still covering her eyes, Amber imagined the rage that must be playing out on her mom's face. Taking in the clothes Amber had thrown everywhere, the overturned jewelry box, the poster of a cat riding a unicorn over a rainbow ripped down and stuffed into the trash can. And, of course, the shredded bed canopy.

The silence grew longer. She'd be grounded for life.

But her mom's warm body sank to the floor next to her. An arm draped over her shoulders. Her mom drew Amber close, enveloping her daughter in the orange and coconut smell of her shampoo.

Amber began to cry.

Her mom just held her, rocking slightly, like she'd done when Amber was little. She mumbled reassuring noises and told her everything would be all right. Even though she didn't know what was wrong. Amber wasn't sure she knew exactly what was wrong either, just that it had finally become too much.

Amber's tears slowly stopped flowing. She snuggled closer to her mom's warmth, sniffed, and wiped her nose with the delicate hem of her dress.

"You ready to tell me what's going on?" her mom asked gently.

"I'm sorry," Amber sighed. "I'm just really angry."

"Why?"

"Everything, I guess?" Amber floundered. The words just weren't there to explain. "Everything is changing. I feel like I'm not the same person anymore and a lot of what I used to do was not only stupid, but horrible."

"Middle school is a big change, honey." Her mom smiled down at her, wiping her eyes.

"No," Amber sniffled. "I mean, yeah, it is, but...I'm finding out how awful all these clothes are..."

"Awful?" her mom asked. "Oh honey, I think they're beautiful. But, you know, it's okay. Sometimes our tastes change. You're just growing up. You can't be our little princess forever. Should we get you some new jeans? With rips in them already? You're young, you can explore all sorts of fun styles before you grow up and have to dress for work. Just not those sweats with big words on the butt, please."

"No, you don't understand." Amber buried her face in her mom's shoulder. "We're destroying the planet and I'm helping."

"I see." Her mom nodded sadly. "It's sad what's happening. But you're just a little girl, Amber. Big problems are for big people. Real change to help the planet has to be done by national governments. We have to vote in people who believe in science and support serious change, and your dad and I are voting in every election. Those problems are too big for a kid."

"But we all have to live here. We have to do our part too. The big people aren't doing enough."

"We drive electric cars, don't eat much meat, and use reusable shopping bags," her mom shrugged. "We recycle when we can and buy organic. I think we're doing a lot. Here, let's get ready to go on our special Girls' Day. That always cheers you up. We still have time to work on your big kid wardrobe — sorry, I mean TEEN wardrobe —

before our hair appointments. I know! Let's go shopping at Bespoke!"

Amber stared blankly ahead. Bespoke. What was she going to do about the internship? Could she really take part in the fashion industry at any level?

Her mom dragged her limp body up, brushed off her dress, and guided her into the silver Tesla. The electric car seemed to hug her sympathetically as her mom drove them to the last place on Earth she wanted to think about.

25

THE LAST PLACE ON EARTH

"*B*ut why won't you go in?" Her mom asked. "You love Bespoke!"

"I just don't feel like it, okay?"

Amber wasn't sure why she let her mom bring her here. Maybe she was hoping for the warm, soothing feeling she always got when she went shopping with Mom. Just the two of them. The cat-in-a-sunbeam feeling Wren had talked about. Maybe she was trying to catch the warm cat. But it was running away and she didn't think she could find it in Bespoke. She'd have to make a decision about the internship soon, but she just wasn't ready to give it up. She wasn't going inside, and she was tired of arguing with her mom about it.

Turning away from the shimmering boutique, she strode towards the consignment store a few stores down, yanking open the door to Bygone. At least here she wouldn't be reminded of the big choice she'd have to make, and maybe shopping here would satisfy her mom.

The artfully arranged racks of hand-me-downs were surprisingly soothing. A ghost of the joy she usually felt walking into a store. Despite her mood, Amber couldn't help but admire the quality and beauty of the clothes around her. Everything was so pretty. Jewels really did choose the best items.

Amber spotted the familiar blue-haired woman behind the counter. "Jewels! I'm glad you're here!"

"Well hello, Science Princess Amber Rosenberg." The woman looked up from a magazine she was reading. "What can I do for you?"

"I need your help," Amber said. Behind her, her mom had gotten distracted by the rack of business attire. "But I don't even know what I need."

Jewels leaned forward, resting her elbows on the counter.

"That sounds serious," she narrowed her eyes playfully.

"Kinda," Amber agreed. "If you have a sec?"

Jewels motioned to a young man in a vest and bow tie. "James, take over here. I have an important customer."

Amber and Jewels walked towards the teen section of the store. Jewels didn't say anything. She waited quietly, straightening some shirts as Amber tried to figure out what to say.

She just wanted to talk to someone, work out her thoughts. A pair of boots caught her attention. They were deep red with black soles and laces. They looked brand new.

"Why would someone sell new boots?" she asked, breaking the silence.

"The oxblood Docs?" Jewels nodded. "Aren't they wonderful? I don't know why anyone would get rid of them so soon. Probably grew out of them before they got a chance to wear them much. If they weren't so small, I'd have bought them myself. Wouldn't have pegged you as a Dr. Martens boot kind of girl, though."

Amber stiffened. "People change."

"Indeed," Jewels nodded.

"Have you ever heard of Vivienne Westwood?" Amber remembered the book Trixie had brought into the Green-house what seemed like decades ago. "Her stuff is totally the opposite of how I've always dressed, everything I thought was fashionable. But for some reason, I love it."

"Oh my gosh," Jewels gushed. "Vivienne Westwood is one of my favorites. She's amazing. You know, she came up through the British punk scene. She never let other people define her. She made punk clothes accessible to regular people without sacrificing her style. She was even knighted by the Queen of England! She's actually DAME Vivienne. There's this great quote of hers. She said some-thing like *My clothes have a story. They have an identity. That's why they become classics. Because they keep on telling a story.*"

"Really?" Amber's eyes widened. "What a great thing to say!"

"I agree." Jewels looked at her shrewdly. "What can I help you with, Science Princess Amber Rosenberg?"

"Just Amber, please," she replied. "Mom and I are shopping. We love shopping together, but today I just don't want to. I've been doing this report and, I mean, no offense since you're working in retail and all, but it's kind of changed my opinion of the whole retail fashion thing. All these clothes, wasted. The clothes I'VE wasted, nature I'VE destroyed. I sort of want to throw up. Rivers, animals, people. Pollution. I just can't bring myself to get more future trash when I have a whole stupid wardrobe at home."

Jewels bent to grab a shirt from the floor and put it back on its hanger. "Then why not just wear something you already have?"

"That's a good question," Amber shrugged. "I should, right? But I don't really like any of what I have anymore. I know I sound like a spoiled brat, but it's like wearing the ghost of a person I'm not. And Mom just loves shopping. My brother's bar mitzvah isn't until February. But Mom likes me to have something new for special occasions, so she's already bugging me to buy something. I'd probably only wear it that one night. It's annoying."

Amber kept talking. She couldn't stop, even as Jewels started leading her to the back of the store. It felt so good to talk to someone who actually listened.

"So then here's the other thing about my current wardrobe," Amber continued. "Everyone keeps thinking I'm stupid just because I wear fancy clothes."

Jewels cringed. "Yeah, sorry about that."

"No, it's not just you. It's, like, everybody. I don't see why people have to constantly focus on my clothes. It gets exhausting." Jewels opened her mouth but Amber talked over her. "And now, suddenly, I don't feel good wearing them and my mom doesn't understand. I'm not sure I understand either, but it's true."

Jewels opened her mouth again but Amber didn't even notice. "On top of that, I'm supposed to do this contest for Bespoke next door, which I really wanted super bad. But now I'm worried because what if creating fashion means I'm causing more dyes to be thrown into rivers and more water to be sucked up? Where will the river otters live then? Huh? Where?!"

Amber stopped walking and realized Jewels had stopped a few steps ago. She watched Amber with a look between seriousness and trying not to laugh.

"What?"

Jewels shrugged. "That's a lot to think about! I thought you just wanted to know the best color to go with your hair!"

"My hair," Amber groaned. "Everybody loves my hair."

"No, seriously, I have totally underestimated you, and I actually think pretty highly of you. I mean, the whole Bespoke internship, of course..."

"Oh yeah!" Amber grinned. "I forgot you knew about that!"

"Of course I do, you know, actually..." Jewels started, but Amber interrupted her again.

"Right! Of course, they're right next door! You probably do lunch with the other employees over there or something right?"

"Employ— uh, yeah, something like that. Anyway, what do you think you're going to do about it? It's a pretty fierce contest, you know."

Amber nodded, deep in thought. "I know, right? I mean, it's everything I ever wanted. Do I want it anymore? What if how I'm feeling is just a phase and I'll regret not trying? It's just so confusing."

"Well, you're going to have to make up your mind soon. I can't help you there," Jewels pulled a satin dress off the rack in front of her. It was almost Amber's size, the same color as the oxblood boots, and was unlike anything in her closet. It had a short, tight skirt and long sleeves. The collar was an off-the-shoulder band of sequins and fake fur. "But Vivienne Westwood says *Buy less. Choose well. Make it last.* This is our used designer section. Plenty of fancy dresses here that you can wear, then sell right back to me, so they get really well worn before hitting the landfill, and no river otters were harmed in the making... at least not this time around."

Jewels held the dress up to Amber and admired her. "You look lovely. But you know, it's up to you. You need to take charge of what you want. What I know about you, Amber Rosenberg, is that you are one smart cookie. Resourceful, clever, and if anyone can figure out what to do with a wardrobe they no longer connect with, it's you. I have faith in you."

"People keep saying they have faith in me," Amber shook her head. "But I don't."

"I bet you do." Jewels handed her the dress. "I bet you know who you are, deep inside, Amber. You just have to let yourself be that person. Be that person on purpose. Even if it's not the person you were yesterday."

Amber blinked up at the blue-haired woman and smiled. She took the dress, sliding her hand along the lovely satin, and turned to a mirror. As she held the dress in front of her, she began to feel like a new Amber.

Maybe that's what she needed. A new Amber.

"THAT'S ALL YOU WANTED, HONEY?" her mom asked as they left Bygone with only a single item. "I'm sorry, I thought shopping would cheer you up. I do like that store though."

"Thanks Mom." Amber pulled open the door to the car. "It did cheer me up. Not in the way I thought, but I think I can at least see the sunbeam my cat is sitting in."

"What are you talking about, honey?" Her mom glanced over at her. When Amber didn't explain, she just shook her head. "Let's get to the salon. We still have time for a nice glass of sparkling water and a look through the magazines before our appointment."

"Right, my hair." Amber ran her fingers through her hair absentmindedly. "Well, like Vivienne Westwood says, choose well, make it last."

~

AMBER SAT in the salon chair, sparkling water in her hand and stylist's cape draped over her shoulders, staring at the mirror.

The stylist picked up locks of long, luxurious auburn hair, folding it on top of her head in a loose, glamorous updo, tendrils softly framing Amber's delicate face.

"What gorgeous hair you have, sweetheart! What are we going to do with it today?"

Amber continued to stare at herself in the mirror, watching her own face grow stronger and more determined by the minute.

Her mom was right. This was going to make her feel better, too. She needed a change. A real change. She needed a new start. She needed to find out who she was, really was, underneath all the beautiful, fancy dresses. Underneath everything.

More to her reflection than to the stylist, she said, "Cut it off. Cut it all off."

26

A NEW CHAPTER?

Kammie, Wren, and Ivy stared at the disaster inside the Greenhouse. The squirrels had struck again last night.

It was Sunday. Kammie, Ivy, and Wren raced to clean up the mess they'd found in the Greenhouse before Amber arrived. After yesterday's freak-out, they were scared Amber might completely fall apart if she saw the destruction. Ivy and Kammie shoveled clothes back into their bags as Wren ran her fingers over the door frame, searching for the best place to finally screw in the hook latch.

She'd get the lock installed today, no matter what. She refused to be outwitted by squirrels.

"Maybe they have a nest somewhere nearby." Ivy looked out the window at the trees outside.

"But how do they get through the door?" Kammie asked. "It doesn't make sen—"

"OH MY GOD," Wren shrieked.

Kammie and Ivy flipped around so fast they almost crashed into each other.

Amber stood in the doorway.

Her hair was gone.

Well, not gone. But it was entirely different.

Chin-length bangs swept to the side. The back was even shorter. Her delicate face looked more pixieish than ever. Previously hidden ears, now visible, sported little gold studs.

And the change went beyond the new hairstyle. She seemed more confident. All the way down to her feet, which were clad in shiny oxblood Doc Marten boots, tied just to the ankle. Above them sparkled the rhinestone hems of Amber's favorite pair of dark blue leggings, which she usually wore under sweeping lengths of fine tulle skirts. Today, however, they were under cut-off jeans shorts. Amber had embroidered a dragon on the front near the seam.

A blue satin tank top was layered over a tight white long-sleeved shirt, peeking out from underneath an old army jacket. The neck of the tight white shirt had been cut out and the edges left ragged. Amber's old pink back-pack hung from her shoulder, stuffed with something soft.

The otherworldly pixie in the doorway looked nothing like their princess. She looked older, more serious, and somehow, surprisingly, just as stylish. Just in a different way. A style that seemed to go beyond her clothes.

"Hi," she smiled. "What happened here?"

She came in and sat down, oblivious to their frozen expressions.

"Gosh," Kammie said quietly. "You look great."

"Thanks." Amber leaned back against the wall, kicking her new boots up onto the top of the potting table. "So do you."

Kammie looked down at herself and blushed. She was just wearing her usual clothes. "You think so?"

Amber blinked. It had been a reflex, just an automatic response. But Kammie really did look nice. She looked happy. She looked comfortable. She looked like she liked the way she looked. She'd never really noticed Kammie's style before.

"Yes, I really do," Amber realized.

Kammie smiled.

"What the what?" Wren shook her head. "Who are you and what have you done with our Amber."

"Do you like it?" Amber giggled. "I'm finding my own style, reworking what I already have. Finding what I like in each of my pieces of clothing, and highlighting it. It's more fun than shopping."

"Does this mean we're back on track to get stuff done?" Ivy asked, putting away the last of the squirrel wreckage.

"Yup. So here's the thing. I don't want to give up fashion. I just don't want to simultaneously destroy the planet," Amber grabbed the Vivienne Westwood book and leafed through it.

"Wait, no. I'm not done talking about this," Wren

frowned, pointing to Amber. "I haven't had time to process, and you want to move on."

"What? I cut my hair and reworked my clothes. But I've still got the same mind under here," Amber said. "Look, we're all growing up. Just like nature, we have to change — to adapt. That's how the strong survive. Become who you need to be today."

"So?" Wren pushed. "What's changed? Because you sure look a lot different than you did yesterday."

"What's changed is what I know now. Everything changes. Just look outside." Amber waved a hand at the skeletal wisteria branches. "The leaves and flowers die and grow back. And it's still wisteria, with or without its flowers. You have to change to grow, right? That's what I realized yesterday."

"And?" Ivy asked. "What does that mean for the competition? We're still doing this, right?"

"Yes," Amber nodded. "If you guys are still in. But we're going to make it mean something, make a statement. Not to win."

"What's the point of entering a contest if you don't try to win?" Ivy scoffed.

"Because! Because we can. Because we have something to say! Because we have a platform to speak and we need to use it. And because it's FUN! Look, this book is all about Vivienne Westwood, an amazing fashion designer." Amber found the page she'd been looking for and read from it. "She says *Fashion is very important. It is life-enhancing and, like everything that gives pleasure, it is worth doing well."*

"Inspiring. Now what does all that actually mean?" Ivy crossed her arms sternly. "Time is running out. We've got to get on it if we're going to make your deadline. Speeches are fine, but we need action, Amber."

Amber showed them a page in the book. It showed the face of an older woman with red hair piled on top of her head. Written across the image were the words, "The only reason I'm in fashion is to destroy the word conformity."

Ivy rolled her eyes, but smirked.

"Okay, first things first." Amber pulled out a notebook. "I did some research into what's being done to help the planet, not just about its problems. Apparently the best thing we can do, especially with clothes, is to stop all the waste. Stop throwing away so much. Last night I went through my wardrobe. I pruned a few things I didn't like anymore and am re-styling the rest. As Vivienne West-wood says..."

Amber flipped through the book again.

"If you do this, something will change. What will change is that you will change, your life will change, and if you can change you, you can, perhaps, change the world. What that means to me is that we all have a part in figuring out how to help the planet. Like this one farmer who learned that feeding his cows a special kind of seaweed, asparasomething taxiformis, reduced the methane in their farts to almost zero. If farmers fed that to their cows instead of corn, it would be like taking hundreds of millions of cars

off the road. Maybe we could use that corn to make bioplastics and compostable plastics so we can stop digging up fossil fuels. Maybe I'll invent compostable corn plastic some day in the future. You never know."

"If anybody can, it's you!" Wren encouraged.

"So," Kammie offered, "you're saying we should all channel our inner Greta Thunberg?"

"I'm saying we should channel our own strengths. Like Greta does, sure. But in our own way. Everyone can play their own part. We're all connected. We can all do SOME-THING. A woman from Kenya, Wangari Maathai, won the Nobel Peace Prize for her ecology efforts. The first woman from any country on the entire continent of Africa to win one. She's planted over ten million trees to prevent soil erosion in Kenya. There are all kinds of people from every part of the globe working to help the earth. Inventing ways to get the plastic out of the oceans and replant trees. People are eating less meat. Vivienne Westwood is making fewer collections and making them only half as large. AND refusing to use any new denim. Another designer named Stella McCartney is heading up a sustainable style movement. Did you know here in America, places like Texas could capture a ton of carbon from the air if their prairie grasses grow back? And it all starts with consuming less."

"But didn't you just get new boots?" Ivy pointed to Amber's feet.

"Yup!" Amber held up her head proudly. "They're used. And this," she hefted the backpack to the top of the table, "is for Trixie. A bunch of clothes that either don't fit or I just can't make work. Where is she?"

"I told her we'd be out trying to repair the squirrel damage before you arrived," Wren shrugged. "She wouldn't come."

"Huh," Amber shrugged. "I'll give them to her later. Meanwhile, here's what I've got for us. We use those."

She pointed to the bags of clothes in the corner.

"But," Kammie squirmed. "A second-hand store rejected them. How can they be nice enough to win a fashion competition? And aren't you supposed to make the stuff yourself?"

"Yes, but we can repurpose them." Amber picked up the ball of Wren's t-shirt yarn. "We aren't going to buy anything new for this Face-Off. Nothing at all. We'll make whatever we need from what we have. Vivienne West-wood says *It's about doing it yourself, buying less and choosing well. Stop sucking things up.* We can cut these up and use the parts we love to make something we love even more."

"Frankenclothes?" Wren grabbed a few handfuls out of a bag and tossed them onto the table. Dresses, skirts, shirts, purses, and a few necklaces.

Ingredients.

"This stuff isn't going to a landfill anymore," Amber said. "It's been overlooked by everyone, even me. But there's something in each piece I loved enough to buy it in the first place. We're going to send a message to the entire fashion industry. Or, at least, the judges. Don't underestimate what you've got! I'm working on designs for each of you to wear in the show based on your personalities and a theme."

She dug through the piles on the tables and, not finding what she wanted, turned and dug through a different bag. Finally, she pulled out a simple, beautiful, teal purse.

"This will be our greatest invention!" Amber held it over her head. "Ivy, THIS is what we'll wire to light up. I've got some ideas."

"Okay," Ivy agreed. "But if you quote Vivienne West-wood one more time, I'm going to scream."

"BAM," agreed Wren. "We're going to SCIENCE the snot out of them."

27

IS ANYONE LISTENING?

"You're done with the report already?" Mrs. Mailloux looked impressed. "You are ready for the presentation?"

Amber passed over three-and-a-half typed, stapled pages titled *The Impact of the Global Fashion Industry*.

It wasn't her best work. Words slapped together. Sources skimmed. But it was done. And she'd poured her passion into it. Getting this information out to as many people as possible was more important to her than a grade. She wanted to give the first presentation so the other kids would pay attention. By the fifth or sixth, they usually zoned out.

"Very well." The teacher wrote her name in the first slot on the whiteboard schedule. "You may present tomorrow."

Amber was surprised to find that she felt ready. She'd expected to feel nervous but didn't.

She felt the eyes of her classmates as they filed into the room and took their seats. Some had already seen her new look, but most hadn't. Emma collided with Tiffanie as they entered, gawking at Amber. Amber had even passed Axel in the hall on the way to class and the blond girl had stopped so suddenly she almost dropped all her books. Amber had waved but Axel just glared and walked off, apparently still mad about the other day. But Amber didn't care. She sat with her head held high, paging through her notes. From the corner of her eye she could see people's shocked expressions.

And she liked it.

"IN CONCLUSION," Amber said as she stood in front of the class, reading from her note cards, "toxic dyes, water use, overcrowded landfills, and the emission of carbon from shipping are some of the biggest culprits making the fashion industry the second largest polluter of the world today. We may look good, but we are making our planet look, and feel, bad." She looked up and met every eye she could.

Silence greeted her final words. A few kids' mouths were hanging open.

"Thank you," she concluded with a nod. "Any questions?"

Again, silence.

Finally, Tiffanie raised a hand. "Why did you cut your hair?"

"Why not," Amber frowned. "Any other questions?"

From the back of the room, Alexander called, "I didn't even know you owned a pair of jeans!"

He snickered. Ivy, sitting next to him, bopped him on the back of the head.

"Any questions about the global fashion industry?" Amber tried one more time.

Emma piped up, "Did you throw away your princess dress? Because isn't that landfill?"

Amber threw up her hands.

"No, I did not throw away my dress. I gave it away. Wait, which dress?" She caught herself. "It doesn't matter. My clothing is not the point I'm trying to make here. Can we talk about what I'm SAYING?"

Suddenly the kids got quiet again as Mrs. Mailloux stood up, clapping.

"Excellent presentation, Miss Rosenberg. Merci." She turned to the rest of the class as Amber walked to her seat. "I hope everyone is just as prepared for their own reports. You must sign up for a presentation slot by the end of the week, if you have not already done so. As you know, there will be no class next week to observe the Thanksgiving holiday. Now, if you'll please open your books to page fifty-two, let's go over last night's homework."

Amber sat down sullenly. Had anyone really listened? Did anyone care? About anything other than her outfit.

Even with an entirely different style, people still only seemed to care about what she wore.

What had she expected? Vibrant discussion? Kids, transformed by the power of her words, throwing off the shackles of mall stores? Not even Mrs. Mailloux had lingered on her actual report. No one was listening.

She'd just have to be content with speaking the truth, whether anyone else listened or not.

28

WORKING THE PLAN

"SHRED IT! KILL IT! DESTROY!" Wren ferociously tore the sleeve off a delicate, butter-colored blouse. "ARGH!"

At least she tried to. The blouse seemed to be fighting back. She tugged and tugged, but the sleeve stayed firmly sewn in place.

"Hang on," she grunted. "This is unexpectedly good workmanship. I'll get it."

Wren yanked harder, her face turning purple. The fabric began to tear a bit, but the seam wouldn't budge. Not even when she grabbed it with her teeth and wrenched it back and forth like a stick of beef jerky.

Defeated, she hung her head.

Kammie offered her a pair of scissors. She took them without looking up, squinting at the chewed-up seam. Amber tossed more clothes on the table in front of her.

"When you've triumphed over the blouse, take the skirt off this dress," instructed Amber.

"Wren smash!" Wren saluted back, stabbing at the blouse with the scissors.

"CAREFULLY."

"If you want careful, get Kammie to do it," Wren mumbled. "I thought you wanted the sheer destruction that only I can bring to the table."

They all had special jobs. A long list of color-coded tasks hung on the wall next to sketches of their outfits. Kammie sorted and matched, Wren disassembled, and Amber and Ivy integrated the sewn circuit into her old teal purse. Making the schedule had taken time, but she knew in the end it would keep them all on track to finish on time. And breaking the tasks down had really helped her understand exactly what needed to get done.

It was strange. Once Amber had decided she didn't care about winning anymore, something inside her had uncorked. Whatever had held her back, it was gone now. The path forward seemed clear. Transforming old clothes was apparently called upcycling. Amber had been surprised to find out it was already a thing.

Everyone worked at their tasks. Amber suddenly realized something was missing. Or, someONE anyway.

"Hey, where's Trixie?" she asked Wren, whose laser-like focus on the blouse had put her into another world. No answer there.

Amber would have to hunt down Trixie later. Right now she and Ivy had a purse to light up.

"Okay, where were we?"

"Installing the circuit in this purse." Ivy opened the flap and looked inside. "It's a good choice. It'll work well."

The purse was rigid and rectangle with a stiff satin flap. The strap was broken, but otherwise it was in great shape. And the clasp was magnetic. Metal. Amber pointed it out to Ivy.

"I see where you're going," Ivy nodded. "If we can connect one end of the circuit to either side of the snap using the conductive thread, it would act as a switch. Snapped, and the electricity flows through and lights up the LED. Unsnapped, and the circuit is broken, the lights go out."

"Great, here's what I want it to look like." Amber spread a drawing next to the purse. "Can you add in where to sew things so it works?"

Ivy compared the purse and the drawing. Three flowers clustered along the side of the flap, with lines coming out that Ivy assumed were supposed to be the glow of LEDs. "So you want three lights on it?"

"Yup," Amber nodded. "Buried inside fabric flowers. I was hoping Trixie could help make the flowers but she's never here anymore."

Ivy set their makeshift battery holder against the inside wall of the purse. "I don't see any problems putting a battery here if we sew it with regular thread, but we'll need more power to run three lights. We'll have to get a real battery holder and some new, bigger batteries. We only have button batteries."

"But we have a lot of those." Amber shook her head. "And we can't get anything new. Is there any way we could work with what we have?"

"I guess," Ivy considered it. "But since we only have one switch, this one clasp, we need to string the lights in a series or parallel circuit and stack the batteries together."

Amber stared at Ivy. "A what now?"

"A series or parallel circuit," Ivy waved dismissively. "You know, like a string of Christmas lights."

"No, I don't know," Amber replied, frustrated. "We celebrate Hanukkah. But I assume you mean fairy lights?"

"Yeah, sorry," Ivy nodded.

"I have no idea how that would work," Amber frowned. "Yet."

"It's not very complicated," Ivy scoffed. "It's not exactly rocket science."

"Hey, that's not fair," Amber frowned. "Just because my mom hasn't been drilling this stuff into me since I was a baby doesn't mean I can't understand it. Yet. I'd like to learn about series and parallel circuits. But right now, can you just make it work?"

"Sure." Ivy looked surprised. "I'm sorry, I didn't mean to imply anything. You know lots of stuff I don't. Like how to sew! I can tell you where to put stuff, but you should really do the sewing. That's what makes us a good team."

Amber relaxed. "Sorry, I didn't mean to snap. I'm just stressed. So much to do, so little time. Yes, please tell me where to sew and I'll do it."

"Gotcha, boss," Ivy replied, pulling the electrical tape

off the makeshift battery holder and stacking two more button batteries on top of the first. The batteries all faced the same way, with all the positive sides facing up, and all the negative sides facing down, positive sides touching negative sides. Then she put one paper clip at the top of the stack and another at the bottom. She rewrapped it all in the electrical tape, tugging tightly to make sure it didn't fall apart. The whole battery bundle went inside the purse. She lightly penciled a path for the conductive thread on the inside of the purse.

Amber looked around for Trixie, then remembered she wasn't there. She might be sticky and occasionally annoying, but Trixie was also a smart kid and they could really use her help. No one else had time to make fabric flowers. Without Trixie, they wouldn't get done. She'd have to think of something else.

One of the laundry bags caught her eye.

"Ah-HA," From the depths of the bag Amber drew out a truly hideous tunic drowning in a sea of fabric flowers of all different colors and sizes. "For you, Ivy!"

"Uhh." Ivy swallowed hard. "You aren't going to make me wear that, are you?"

"You don't like it?" Amber hid a teasing smile behind the fabric. "Models don't have to actually LIKE the designs they wear."

Ivy coughed and tried to smile.

"I'm just teasing," Amber laughed. "It's hideous. But look at how pretty the flowers are! They'll go great on the purse."

"Oh! Thank goodness," Ivy sighed, looking closer at the flowers. "Great idea, these'll work. We can stick the LEDs right in the middle. Will the flowers come off in one piece?"

A giant rip came from behind them followed by Wren's evil laughter. "Take that, Butter Shirt! You're no match for the mighty Wren."

The delicate yellow sleeve fluttered onto Amber's shoulder.

"Great timing." Amber handed the flowered shirt to Wren. "Please surgically remove these flowers, doctor."

Wren threw back her head with another wild laugh and tossed it onto her pile.

"How are you doing, Kammie?" Amber asked.

"Fine." Kammie sat inside a rainbow of fabric, sorted neatly into piles by color and clothing type. "You sure have a lot of blue dresses. I thought there'd be more pink."

"I love blue," Amber shrugged.

Ivy waved the conductive thread in front of Amber's face, "Hey, pay attention here. I can't sew!"

"Yet!" Amber responded, turning back to Ivy. "But, here give it to me."

Silence descended over the Greenhouse as clothes met their doom, and tasks were checked off. Scissors flashed wildly as the four of them sorted, sewed, and planned. They were making good headway, but something was still missing.

"Darn it, I wish Trixie were here," Amber groaned. "Why isn't she helping?"

"Don't ask me." Wren tugged at a fabric flower. "She

refuses to come out to the Greenhouse anymore. I think she's scared of the squirrels."

Amber paused. Trixie was essential to the plan. Not just to help them work, but as a model, too. Trixie's outfit was one of Amber's favorites, made from strip after strip of the finest fabrics in her collection, torn and left ragged on the edges. Wild and unrefined, made of beautiful potential. Just like Trixie.

Without her, the whole fashion line didn't make as much sense. Trixie represented the future, and her outfit was supposed to represent the decision between landfill and less waste. It was the finale of Amber's presentation. She needed her.

"I'll have to go get her," Amber mused.

"Why?" Wren continued to rip flowers off the shirt, most of them falling apart as she pulled. "She's being stupid. I tried. The squirrels haven't done anything we couldn't fix. It's not like they've ever come in while we were here."

"Yet," Amber added distractedly. "I'll try to convince her. Be right back."

"Amber!" Ivy called. "We're not done with the circuit!"

"Be right back!" she called again, heading out the door.

Trixie sat on the couch, surrounded by stacks of paper and a pile of jackets. A long chain of finger knitting wrapped several times around her arm, and Trixie continued to work at it diligently. She'd changed out several different colors and textures throughout its length.

She was just reaching the end of green when Amber walked in.

"Hey there." Amber pushed the jackets aside and flopped next to her.

Trixie frowned and shifted, turning her back to Amber.

"What's up?" Amber tried again.

Trixie turned farther away and yanked the thread over her fingers again and again.

"Hmmm. I think somebody needs a tickle!" Amber's fingers wiggled at Trixie's sides. A smile and a frown fought on Trixie's face. The frown won.

"Okay, enough. What's going on?"

More silence. The chain continued to grow off the back of Trixie's hand. Amber looked at her watch in exasperation.

"I need you, Trix," Amber said. "Please come out to the Greenhouse, okay? I have to get back to help the others."

As Amber started back down the hallway toward the backyard, Trixie yelled after her.

"NO!"

Amber didn't know what else to do. Even the new latch didn't seem to make her feel safer. They were really making progress, and Amber didn't have time to deal with more stupid squirrel attacks or frightened six-year olds. Maybe if they could go a few days without an attack, she'd join them again. And they certainly couldn't afford any more setbacks.

Amber would just have to make extra sure the latch was locked when they left tonight.

Sewn Circuit (part 2)

Conductive thread
Electrical tape
1 Large-eyed embroidery needle
2-3 Coin cell (button) battery
2-3 LEDs (same amount as batteries)
Sew in metal snap (preferably magnetic)
Strip of fabric that fits around your wrist

CR2032
+

Tip: Make sure the tails of your stitched paths don't touch or you could short your circuit!

Tip: TEST EACH LED before sewing it down to make sure you have the right polarity.

Tip: Sew one snap on the back of the fabric so they hook up correctly.

Series Circuit:

In a **series circuit**, electricity runs through each component, one after the other, like the baton in a relay race: the battery passes electricity to a light, who takes it, runs, then passes it to another light, who takes it, runs, and passes it, all the way back to the battery.

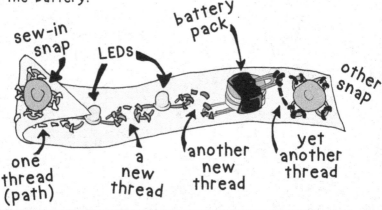

sew-in snap

LEDS

battery pack

other snap

one thread (path)

a new thread

another new thread

yet another thread

Prepare Components:

Stack 3 batteries on top of each other, keeping the positive sides all facing up. Put a paperclip on each side and wrap snuggly in electrical tape.

Tape

Thread and knot your needle like you did in the first sewn circuit.

Bend the legs of the LEDs so they loop and lay flat.

Parallel Circuit:

In a **parallel circuit**, electricity runs through each SIDE of each component in one long path, like it's on conveyor belts. One belt comes from the positive side of the battery. The other goes back to the negative side. All the LED's positive leads touch the positive conveyor belt, and the negative leads touch the negative belt.

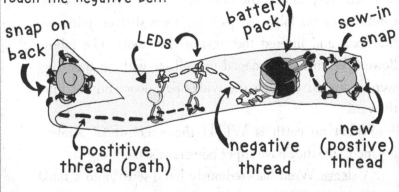

snap on back

LEDs

battery pack

sew-in snap

postitive thread (path)

negative thread

new (postive) thread

29

SCIURUS GRISEUS ZOMBIKUS

"*H*ow did they get IN, darn it!?" Amber looked around the fresh wreckage on Sunday. Luckily, since Ivy couldn't meet because of some basketball team thing, she'd taken the sewn circuit purse home with her. Amber would have been beyond devastated if the nasty little rodents had destroyed it.

Wren ran her fingers along the door frame and flipped the hook on the latch. This was no ordinary squirrel. They had definitely locked the door yesterday. Now, stacks of carefully sorted fabric strips hung from shelves, piled on the floor, and littered the tops of the stools. The fabric flowers Wren had managed to pull off without breaking were scattered through the wide-open door and out into the yard.

"What on earth is WITH these monsters?" Amber groaned. "Do they have super powers or something?"

A sleeve Wren had tediously hand-sewn onto a tank

top under Amber's frustrated supervision had been torn back off. It draped over an upside-down paper cup while a nearby stool wore the tank top part. Amber sat heavily on top of it.

Kammie sniffed back tears as she diligently gathered the remnants of her meticulously color-coded piles of fabric strips.

"Why?" Kammie choked. "Why would squirrels even do something like this?"

"Squirrels didn't do this," Wren said resolutely from the doorway. "There is no way a normal squirrel could have unlocked this latch. No, this isn't the work of an ordinary squirrel. Unlocking this door would take a lot more patience and persistence than any squirrel possesses."

Amber shook her head. "What else could it possibly be?"

"Sabotage," Wren offered.

The other two stared at her. Kammie looked worriedly at Amber, who shook her head.

"No. No way. Who on earth would sabotage my collection?" She tossed another few scraps to Kammie. "Even if anyone thought that I actually posed some kind of threat, for some reason, no one knows I'm working back here. It's not even the address on my application!"

"You're right," Wren agreed. "It would have to be someone who could see into this yard. Have you seen any drones around?"

"Be serious," Amber snipped.

"I am being serious. Honestly, the only thing running

around this yard besides us is squirrels and some crows. And like I said, it would take a very unusual squirrel to..."

Wren went silent.

"What is it?" Kammie asked quietly.

"Oh no," Wren looked at the others with wide, frightened eyes. "Oh no. Guys. I know what it is."

"What?" said Kammie and Amber together.

"It's not squirrels. It's...no," her voice dropped to a whisper. "But yes. It has to be. It can only be...zombie squirrels."

"What?!?" yelled Amber. "What are you even talking about?"

"ZOMBIE SQUIRRELS!" Wren yelled back, grabbing her by the shoulders. "Slow, methodical, zombified squirrels with that single-minded obsession zombies get. Only, instead of hungering for brains — they want your designs!"

Amber pushed her off and dropped onto a stool, looking around the wreckage of the Greenhouse helplessly.

"Wren," she buried her head in her arms. "It's not zombie squirrels."

But Wren was pacing, growing frantic. "It HAS to be zombie squirrels, that's the only possible explanation. Does anyone know a defense against zombie squirrels?"

"It's not zombie squirrels, for heaven's sake," Amber's arms muffled her voice.

"All the same," Kammie whimpered. "I'd feel better working in the house from now on."

"Good idea. There's no telling what a zombie squirrel would do if we actually walked in on it. Trixie's right to be

scared," panic crept into Wren's voice. "WHAT ARE WE
GOING TO DO?"

"WREN," screamed Amber. "It's not stupid ZOMBIE
SQUIRRELS, for heaven's sake!"

"How do you know?" Wren asked.

"Because," Amber snipped. "There's no such thing as
zombie squirrels. No one in the history of ever has EVER
seen a zombie squirrel!"

Wren held up her finger and looked Amber in the eyes,
"Yet..."

30

SQUIRRELPOCALYPSE, OR NOT

"The Face-Off is in two weeks, and we can't afford any more setbacks," Amber declared at lunch that Monday. "Since there's only two days of school this week with Thanksgiving and all, maybe we can keep a better eye on the Greenhouse. I don't want to take any chances. Wren, you duct-taped the latch, right?"

Wren nodded, her mouth stuffed full of bagel.

"I still don't understand why they're messing with the projects." Ivy scratched her neck. "It doesn't make sense."

"Zombie squirrels follow no rhyme or reason, Ivy. They live for one single-minded purpose." Wren wiped the cream cheese off her mouth. "To destroy."

"Could we bring stuff home?" Kammie suggested.

"There's too much stuff." Amber sipped from her water bottle. "Besides, all our tools and materials are in the Greenhouse. I don't think we can move it all."

"And even if we did," Wren grabbed some lettuce with

her hand and stuffed it into her mouth, "they'd just destroy everything else in there. They hunger, these zombies do."

Amber and Kammie ignored her.

"What?" Wren crunched. "They do!"

Ivy tore a piece off her biscuit and threw it at Wren. It bounced off her forehead and rolled away, stopping near the fence. A squirrel darted out from nowhere and ran off with it.

Wren pointed to the squirrel as it carried off the biscuit, raising her eyebrows meaningfully at Ivy. As if the biscuit theft proved her entire point. Ivy rolled her eyes.

"We need to catch them in the act," Wren frowned. "We need proof. What if we're at ground zero of the squir-relpocalypse? We have a moral duty to tell the world!"

Ivy tapped her lips. "You're right about one thing. We really do need to get to the bottom of it. But how?"

"Oh, I know!" Wren dug around in her backpack and pulled out the digital camera they'd gotten to catch the election thief. "A stakeout! We can be spies again."

"I can't be a spy," Kammie replied. "I have swim lessons."

Wren narrowed her eyes. "All break?"

"Well," Kammie shrugged. "We're meeting Wednesday, I'm in Tahoe for Thanksgiving and back on Sunday, when I have my swim lessons. So, I don't know when I'll have time to be a spy."

"How about the rest of us do a sleepover Friday night? Tell Mom it's a campout in the backyard." Wren dropped her voice to a loud whisper. "She'd freak if she heard we were hunting zombie squirrels. She doesn't understand that we're seasoned field agents."

"Would your mom let you DO that?" Kammie blinked, surprised. "My mom would never let me sleep in the backyard."

"Sure," Wren shrugged. "Why not? She'll say something like 'wear warm pajamas' though. Totally annoying."

"I don't think I can either," Ivy apologized. "We're going to my grandparents for Thanksgiving, remember? That's why I can't come Wednesday. We'll be back Saturday night."

"You're fired," Wren pouted.

Ivy punched her in the shoulder.

"Well," Amber mused as she began to pack her lunch away, "we aren't going anywhere this year. Just us and Granny at our place. I'm sure I can stay overnight on Friday. Let's give it a try. Meanwhile, does anybody have any new ideas on what IS attacking the Greenhouse, or why?"

"And where did the zombie squirrels even come from?" Wren added.

"Let's get logical. What do we know?" Amber ticked off some facts with her fingers. "The attacks started with the Fashion Face-Off. They only happen when we're not around. What else?"

"The culprit was able to get past the latch on the door," Ivy added. "And they haven't messed with anything except the projects."

"Oh that's true, isn't it?" Kammie gasped. "Nothing but

the projects have been touched. Maybe it is sabotage after all."

"I have to admit sabotage sounds more reasonable all of a sudden," Amber agreed. "What else could it be?"

Wren just looked at her.

Amber sighed.

"Oh!" Wren added. "They only seem to swarm at night."

"Swarm?" Ivy zipped her lunchbox.

"Zombies swarm, Ivy. That's what you call it. Don't you watch movies?" Wren shook her head with exasperation. "Anyway I'll ask Mom at dinner tonight. As long as we promise to wear warm pajamas, I'm sure she'll be fine with it. We have an awesome tent."

Amber looked at her watch. They had a few more minutes. "Meanwhile, I want to talk about the next steps. Kammie, while you're in Tahoe, can you make some milk plastic beads? I made you a color chart."

Kammie nodded. "Shouldn't be a problem."

"Great, so on Wednesday I want to do an experiment. I found some great outfits to pull pieces from, but they're all white or cream-colored, which isn't going to work with my idea."

"So, dye them," Ivy announced. "Problem solved. Why make it complicated?"

"Exactly, except I don't want to buy anything new," Amber pointed out. "And besides, the dyeing part of fashion is horrible for the environment. Totally toxic, and it gets into the water supply."

"Is there a natural way to dye clothes?" Kammie asked.

"That's exactly what I was wondering," Amber agreed. "How do you dye clothes naturally? I mean, people have been dyeing clothes forever and modern toxic dyes have only been around a little while. There have to be ways."

"It's not hard at ALL to stain your clothes," Wren assured her.

"Yup. You should see my little brother's pants," Amber nodded. "Dyeing shouldn't be that hard, considering how easy it is to stain clothes if you drip coffee, or tea, or spaghetti sauce on them."

"Right? Then your dad is all like 'what were you THINKING?' and your mom kind of sighs," Wren groaned. "And then you have to decide if you're going to wear stained clothes or throw out an otherwise perfectly good shirt, so then you decide to keep it as play clothes but you have too many of those, and—"

"Yeah, like that," Amber interrupted. "What about using plants?"

"Like grass?" Wren pointed to the greenish knees of her faded jeans.

"Why not?" Amber pulled a few sketches out of her backpack and laid them on the table. "It's for Kammie's outfit, based on her theme."

Kammie ran a hand lightly over the drawing and a soft, wistful smile crept across her face. "Is this me?"

Amber nodded. "You're *Colorful*. So I want to dye the fabric."

"Me? Colorful? Really?" Kammie said quietly, gazing

at the picture, her eyes brimming with a hint of tears. "You really think of me like that? I love it."

Her reaction caught Amber by surprise. "Well, yeah. Yeah, I do. You may not be flamboyant, but there's so much color to you, Kammie."

Kammie looked up into Amber's eyes and sniffled.

Such a simple thing affected Kammie so strongly. Amber was realizing more and more that words really matter. Not just other people's words to her, but what she said and did too. The words and the thoughts behind them. Unintentional insults, casually thrown out, but also little compliments and speaking honestly. The magic behind simple words like *yet*.

They all had power. And not only her words, but her actions mattered too. The truth behind her words and actions. Using her own skill to pull out a bit of the quiet girl's hidden soul and show it to others. That was a powerful feeling.

Then, behind Kammie, she saw the unmistakable forms of Axel and Milo coming out of the school. Together. Well, sort of together. Milo walked first and Axel followed him. He said something sharply to her and immediately turned to go back into the school, leaving Axel alone on the sidewalk. She looked angry.

Suddenly, a thought struck her. Could it be Axel? Could she be the one destroying their work? Would she really do something like that? She'd proven she could do really selfish things, make really bad choices, and not care about the consequences. It was why they were no longer friends. A warm anger surged through Amber. The more she thought about it, the more she knew she was right. She had to put an end to it this minute. They had too much to do in too little time for any more visits from jealous ex-friends.

"Hey, guys." Amber hurriedly shoved her lunch things back in her backpack. "I have something I need to take care of. I'll see you later."

Over by the door, kids moved in and out of the school. Axel leaned against the wall looking down at her feet. Alone. Amber stopped in front of her, hands on her hips, and waited.

Axel looked up. Then she looked away.

"What do you want now?" she asked Amber sadly.

"Is it you?" Anger crept into Amber's voice. "Are you the one messing everything up?"

Axel looked at her, confused. "What is that supposed to mean?"

"You." Amber thrust a finger at her. "You're destroying my chances to win the competition. You can't handle that I got in and you didn't. And you need to stop."

Axel's eyebrows pulled together in more confusion. She didn't say anything. It just made Amber angrier.

"I don't know what you're talking about." Axel pushed herself away from the wall. "I'm leaving."

Surprising herself, Amber found her hand pushing Axel back against the wall. Like she'd lost control of her own body.

"No, we're talking about this now." The power in

Amber's voice shocked her. "This has to stop. No more attacks on the Greenhouse, do you understand? I only have two more weeks. We're trying to do something important. I can't have you sabotaging everything just because you're jealous."

They stared at each other. Amber felt a rush of power. A pride in her own confidence, her action. She wouldn't be shoved around anymore. She was done apologizing.

But suddenly tears began to form in Axel's pale blue eyes. She swept Amber's hand off her shoulder and stepped away.

"What do you want from me?" Axel's voice wavered. "I get it, I messed up! You're not my friend anymore. Milo and Bobby won't even talk to me. NOBODY talks to me. I said I was sorry! Why won't anyone give me a second chance?"

Amber froze. What? "You mean, it's not you? You're not the one who keeps destroying my designs?"

"Why would I do that?" Axel cried. "I don't care about your stupid designs. Good luck to you, I'm sure you deserve it. But why do you always think such bad things about me? I made a mistake. Isn't anyone ever going to forgive me? I'm not some villain, Amber. I have more important things to do than worry about your stupid amazingness. Not everything is about YOU."

The perky blond ponytail flipped in Amber's face as Axel turned and raced toward the door, sobbing.

Amber watched her go in horror. She'd been wrong. And mean. And now she'd hurt someone. How could she do that? Thinking back to how Ivy had hurt her earlier, Amber cringed. Her words, her actions could be used to hurt people. That power, the power of words and actions, it was a responsibility too.

And something else kept bothering her. If Axel wasn't the one destroying everything, who was it? Could it actually be the start of the squirrelpocalypse after all?

31

DYEING FOR FASHION

Orange peels, beet skins, a few cranberries, and other fruits and vegetables tumbled onto Wren's kitchen table the day before Thanksgiving. Amber shook the bag to make sure it was empty. A glass spice jar full of some yellowy-orange powder rolled out.

"Your salad looks disgusting." Wren wrinkled her lip. "I'm gonna stick to popcorn."

Amber tossed a pair of thick white knee socks in the middle of the food scraps.

"Now I'm really not hungry," Wren gagged. "Why are you dumping your compost all over the table?"

Amber, Kammie, and Wren clustered in Wren's kitchen for their dyeing experiment. Ivy was already at her grandparents' house.

The kitchen was bright, sunny, and sparkling clean. In the corner, at a little play table, Trixie chewed on the remains of a peanut butter sandwich, endlessly pulling yarn over her fingers. Following the sequence, over and over again. She didn't look up as the girls began their experiment.

"Hey Trix," Amber smiled. "We're working inside today. No squirrels! Are you going to come join us?"

Trixie grabbed her plate sullenly, dumped it in the sink, and walked out without saying a word.

Wren groaned. "She's so annoying."

Amber made a mental note to go check on her later. The same note she'd been making for days, but hadn't gotten around to. She just didn't have time.

"Okay," Amber began. "I did some research. There are a ton of different ways to dye clothes naturally, but the process is mostly the same. The colors and how strong they are depend on a lot of variables, like what material you're dyeing, the plant or vegetable you use, how long you let it cook, and the fixative you use."

"Cook?" Kammie asked, as Amber piled more clothes on the table next to the socks. "Mom doesn't let me use the stove unless she's in the room."

"Well, you cook the dye," Amber replied. "That's why I wanted to work in the kitchen. I hope it's okay if we use the stove. Then when you put the clothes in, I guess soak would be a better word. Or brew. The clothes have to sit in the dye for a long time. Do you have any buckets?"

"MOM, WE'RE GONNA MAKE A MESS IN THE KITCHEN," Wren yelled. Amber and Kammie winced. "I don't know about buckets. We may have to use bowls. We have a few big pots for the cooking part, though."

Wren dug through the cupboards as a muffled reply from her mom drifted to them from some other part of the house.

"What did she say?" Kammie asked hesitantly.

Wren shrugged. "No idea."

"So I thought we'd use the scientific method to determine what gives us the best results." Amber began sorting through the vegetable and plant leftovers she'd brought. She pulled a pencil and a slightly damp spiral notebook from her bag. "Experiment, observe, and come to a conclusion. We can test out a few dyes and observe and record the results. Then use what works best. I made a chart."

"Is there a difference between the scientific method and the engineering design process?" Wren asked. "They seem pretty similar. I mean, they both start with a question, include research, and end with an answer. Except I guess an engineer's answer is a thing, and a scientist's answer is an idea, right?"

"I think the difference is that a scientist is answering a question by observing what happens, and an engineer is inventing a solution for a problem," Amber guessed.

Wren squinted at the food scraps, trying to see them without touching anything. "What do you have?"

"I grabbed a bunch of leftover stuff from our kitchen. That spice in the jar there, that's turmeric. It's supposed to make a great yellow dye."

Wren, rooting around in the fridge, pulled out a container of blackberries. "These are getting a little moldy. Should we use them?"

"Do we want moldy fruit on our clothes?" Kammie asked.

"I think the boiling water should kill the mold," Amber pointed out. "Let's try it."

"Why do plants come in different colors anyway?" Kammie held up a beet skin, which immediately started staining her fingers red.

"Good question!" Wren reached for her iPad. "I'll do some research."

As she jabbed at the screen, Amber and Kammie began to sort the food scraps by color.

"The type of fabric is super important," Amber said. "It has to be a natural fiber because dye won't stick to a synthetic fiber very well. They had to invent synthetic dyes, because they invented synthetic fibers. So I had to choose wool, cotton, silk, stuff like that."

"Hey!" Wren piped up. "Did you know a scientist in Australia is inventing cotton that grows in colors, instead of just white? If she's successful, we won't have to dye it at all!"

"Seriously?" Amber pulled two gigantic plastic bins from another bag. They were large and sloshed when she moved them like there was liquid inside. They had masking tape labels, with the words SALT and VINEGAR on them. "That's cool."

Kammie looked over Wren's shoulder. "Weren't you looking up why plants are different colors?"

"But it was interesting," Wren shrugged.

"Try to stay focused." Kammie turned back to the table. "So what do we do?"

"It's pretty simple." Amber set the bins on the table. "We chop up anything we want to use as a dye and stew it in water for a while. I already simmered the clothes in fixative for an hour."

"Fixative sounds like something that would take the stain out." Kammie started filling the pots with water. "You know, fix it?"

"No, it's something that helps the fabric hold a color, so it doesn't wash out. Like fix it in place. There are lots of natural fixatives, like alum, which is this weird white powder we have in our spice rack. But I used salt and vinegar." Amber pointed to the plastic containers.

"How did you fixative them?" Wren asked, cracking open the one that said vinegar. She wrinkled her nose and immediately sealed it again. "Yuck! That stinks."

"You should have smelled it while it was cooking!" Amber looked at her notes. "For the vinegar one, I used a ratio of four cups of water to one cup of vinegar, and the salt one has eight cups of water to half a cup of salt. I guess salt is stronger since you dilute it more? Dunno. I made both because they say to use vinegar with plant dyes and salt with fruit dyes. I guess I could have used the alum stuff with either, but they say you shouldn't use the pot for food afterwards if you make an alum mordant with it. And mom said no."

"Mordant?" Wren looked up.

"Fixative. Same thing." Amber replied. "Anyway, I

added the clothes and let them simmer for an hour on the stove. Then I let them cool and put the wet clothes in these plastic things to bring here, because the clothes are supposed to be wet when you add them to the dye bath."

Wren giggled. "A bath to get you dirty instead of clean."

Kammie pulled out some cutting boards while Amber filled the pots with water and turned on the stove. Wren set aside the iPad and helped chop up the food waste. Then they carefully slid the chopped food into the pots, but the water splashed out anyway.

"We should have added the food BEFORE adding the water," Kammie pointed out, wiping at the spills with a rag.

"You're going to set that rag on fire." Wren took it from her and tossed it into the sink, picking up her iPad again. "Trust me."

Four mismatched pots simmered away happily. One held a bunch of beet skins and crushed cranberries. The turmeric and onion skins were in another. Red cabbage simmered in the third pot with the blueberries. That one smelled disgusting, so Kammie turned on the fan above the stove. The last one just had plain water. Amber started digging through their scraps for a new color to add.

"Oh, listen to this!" Wren read from a website.

"Is it why plants are different colors?" Kammie asked.

"Not exactly. It's about people seeing colors. Christine Ladd-Franklin, a scientist born back in 1847, was a mathematician and psychologist and — well, she did a lot of stuff. Wow, she was really amazing. But anyway, she came up with this theory that people didn't just start seeing color all at once. She thought humans started out only seeing black and white. Then we evolved to see blue and yellow, and then red and green. Which is why some people are color-blind. Especially red and green color-blind. Because it's a kinda new trait. My grandpa is color-blind."

"That's fascinating," Kammie said. "But did you find out why plants are different colors?"

Wren looked at her apologetically. "Ummm."

"Can you look it up later?" Amber set the iPad out of Wren's reach. "I'd like to get these clothes dyed."

"What are we putting in the last pot?" Wren peered into them.

"I'm not sure." Amber held up some celery. "I don't even know why I brought this. I doubt it will work."

"Let's do grass!" Wren yanked open the sliding door to her yard. Most of the grass was brown, dead for the winter.

"I don't think dead grass will work," Amber mused. "I think the dye sucks the color from whatever is in the water, so maybe something else green?"

"Let's get as much green grass as we can find," Wren pulled kitchen scissors from a drawer. "And maybe we can throw in some of the plant leaves. They're green too."

"Why not?" Amber agreed. "It's all an experiment!"

Wren harvested a few handfuls of green plant matter, cut it up, and dumped it into the pot.

"Once we see what dyes best, we can sew the best pieces together." Amber swished around the plastic containers. "I have a lot of options in each kind of fixative, but we have to let the dye baths cook for like an hour before they're ready."

Steam crept up from the four pots and filled the room, despite the stove fan running full tilt. It smelled horrible. Wren opened a window, but it didn't help much. After an hour of simmering, though, the liquids looked nice and colorful.

They strained the solid pieces out of the dye baths, throwing them in the compost bin.

"Okay, now we soak the clothes in the dye for as long as possible," Amber read from her notes. "We can turn off the stove. Here's where the buckets would come in handy."

Wren pointed to some mixing bowls. "These are all I can find. Will they work?"

"In order to compare the results, we need to label everything." Kammie stuck labelled masking tape to the bowls as Wren set them on the counter. "Otherwise we won't know our results."

"The pots are probably too hot to put on the counter." Wren pulled a ladle from a drawer. "Maybe we can transfer the dye into the bowls with this?"

Wren handed the ladle to Kammie and held the bowl near the stove. Kammie diligently scooped a few ladlefuls of deep purple liquid into one, but it splashed onto the stovetop. Wren brought the half-filled bowl to the counter, trying not to let the liquid slosh out too much. It still covered her shirt.

"Good thing I wore work clothes," Wren sighed. "But I don't think these bowls will be big enough."

"Maybe we can put the fabric right into the pots?" Kammie suggested.

They squeezed the dripping clothing pieces out and added them to the cooling pots. There wasn't anywhere to set the pots so they had to leave them on the stove.

"I hope it's not too hot or anything," Wren said.

"I think it's okay," Amber decided. "In another few hours, they'll be ready!"

"Hours?" Wren pinched her nose. "I think I'm gonna throw up."

They heard footsteps from the hallway.

"WHOA! HOLY..." Wren's mom froze in the doorway. "What's going on? What a MESS!"

The girls looked up in surprise.

"We have to start dinner." Wren's mom sounded frantic. "Are those all my pots? Tomorrow is THANKSGIVING, for heaven's sake. Your dad was going to start some chicken stock tonight. Oh my god. And my bowls. Are there any bowls left?"

The girls looked around. The spotless kitchen had been attacked by squirrels after all. But this time, THEY were the squirrels.

Bits of food covered the table. Juice puddled on the counters, on the tabletop, and dripped onto the floor. Knives, pots, cutting boards, and strainers littered the counters. Drawers hung open. Dye splattered the stovetop. Water droplets trailed from the sink to the pots and bowls.

It looked like the aftermath of a tornado.

"Oh, sorry," Wren swallowed. "It was an accident."

"An accident? This isn't an accident, Wren! This is a catastrophe! Do you know how long it took us to clean this kitchen?" Wren's mom battled to remain calm. She covered her face with her hands. Amber could hear her taking deep breaths. "What were you thinking?"

"It's my fault, Mrs. Sterling." Amber felt awful. "But I promise we'll clean it up. Do you need the pots? Should we move them to the concrete patio outside? Put them on hot pads, maybe?"

"Sure. Whatever." Wren's mom closed her eyes and turned away. "Just have it cleaned up as soon as you can, okay? I swear, Wren, I can't leave you alone for ten minutes without you destroying something. What am I going to do with you, child?"

Wren's mom walked away heavily, calling over her shoulder. "I'll be back in ten minutes. I guess we'll have to order delivery tonight."

"Whoops." Wren's voice sounded strangled, like she was trying not to cry.

"I sort of forgot that doing a good experiment means taking care of your workspace," Amber choked as she watched Wren try to hide her face behind her hair.

"I always clean up after myself," Kammie whispered with embarrassment. "Mom says it's my responsibility to keep my workspace clean if I want the privilege of messing it up. I would have cleaned up."

Amber and Kammie carefully transferred everything to the patio and turned back to the disaster of a kitchen. No one said anything else as they began to scrub all the surfaces. A sob escaped from under Wren's curtain of hair. To Amber, it was just a mistake. But Wren made a lot of mistakes. She didn't mean to, they just sort of happened. Amber knew that Wren tried so hard, but people told her all day long how much she was doing everything wrong. Sometimes Wren just couldn't deal with the criticism, especially when she knew she really had done something wrong. And this time it wasn't even her fault. Amber reached over to touch her shoulder, but Wren pulled away.

"Don't," she said.

Amber froze in uncertainty. She had misjudged Axel, ignored Trixie, and now she'd gotten Wren in trouble and destroyed all her mom's cleaning, messing up their dinner plans. They should have been more careful. She should have planned better.

But she hadn't. She'd messed up.

It was her duty to make it right.

Natural Dye

Materials:

Salt
Large Pots
Buckets/bowls
Strainer
White vinegar

Other Materials:

Clean light colored natural fabric:
(cotton, linen, silk, etc)

Food leftovers or plant scraps:
(beets, red cabbage, onion skins, grass,
flowers, spinach, blueberries, spices, etc!)

Fixative (Mordant)

For PLANTS, try 2 cups vinegar
to 8 cups water. For FRUIT, try
1/2 cup salt to 8 cups water.

Simmer
clothes
in fixative
for an hour,
then wring
out and
add to dye.

Dye

Add the food or plant
scraps to a pot with a
gallon of water. Bring to a
boil, then reduce heat. Let
simmer for about an hour
until the color is strong.
Strain out solid pieces.

BE CAREFUL! DYE STAINS! KEEP YOUR WORKSPACE CLEAN!

Add damp clothes to the dye, preferably in a
bucket. Let sit for several hours. Overnight
is even better! The longer it soaks, the
strong the color will be. Remove from the
dye and rinse until the water runs clear.

32

THE STAKEOUT

*T*he tent glowed in the middle of Wren's backyard on Friday night, illuminated from the inside by a lantern nestled between two bulging sleeping bags. Outside the tent, occasional scratching and rustling could be heard over the drone of cars and the occasional muted thunder of a cable car rumbling down nearby Market Street.

Wren clutched her camera and nestled further into her sleeping bag. She hadn't realized how good her house's windows were at keeping out the street noise. They could even hear a distant foghorn blaring every once in a while way out in the bay.

The fog must be thick around the Golden Gate Bridge tonight. It wasn't quite cold enough for them to see their breath, but it certainly wasn't warm once the sun went down. Wren was glad she'd worn her warm pajamas after all.

It probably would have been smarter to set the tent up somewhere hidden, but there really wasn't anywhere to go in the small yard. And they should turn off the lantern if they really wanted to catch whatever was attacking the Greenhouse. They'd tried but had only lasted a few minutes in the dark before turning the light back on.

Amber hadn't been camping before, but she'd seen a lot of movies about it. It looked easy enough. Set up a tent in the wilderness under a giant full moon, oooh and aaaah over the bright stars, maybe cuddle next to your parents as they point out the Milky Way, roast marshmallows over a campfire and tell spooky stories, right? Only it wasn't exactly working out like it did in the movies. The San Francisco fog covered any stars they might have been able to see over the city's light pollution, there was no campfire, and even the moon was just a sliver.

They did have marshmallows though.

Amber had been to a lot of places on vacations. She'd traveled to Europe, Mexico, Canada, and Hawaii. They usually stayed in nice hotels or at a resort on a warm beach. She'd scampered after lizards and tried to identify colorful birds, stuck a snorkeling mask into the water and seen wild sea turtles and exotic fish darting in and out of coral structures.

She'd wandered through forests of giant trees so tall she couldn't see their tops, and dug through decaying leaves, sending bugs scurrying away in all directions as she investigated their roots. She'd wiped humidity from her face as the air itself seemed wetter than the ocean, right before warm rain started to patter against the forest canopy. Rain that only made its way to the forest floor when the pounding of drops grew loud and hard. While her brothers screamed and laughed and ran for the car to avoid the thick drops, she'd made her way slowly, getting drenched, not caring that her mom would yell at her for soaking the seats of the rental car. She'd smelled the rain rising from fresh earth and felt leaves squishing under her feet as they turned into rich soil, changing, evolving, moving to their next purpose. The only sounds had been the rain and a few birds calling to each other after her family had retreated to the shelter of the car.

She'd watch nature change and grow, becoming brand new moment by moment. The cycle of life, actively spinning.

But she'd never camped out in a backyard in the City.

The very city where she lived.

A cable car rumbled again in the distance, miles of steel tracks under its wheels. A muted car horn honked.

Strange that she could lie here, without real walls or a roof, on a field of grass, and be more aware of the urbanness that surrounded her than when she drove around in a car. She thought about the paved streets, the glow of streetlights, the smell of tailpipes. House after house piled on top of each other. People wandering around at all hours. She could hear some now, laughing their way between the bars and restaurants of Market Street.

Her cousins, who lived in a suburb, didn't walk anywhere. They stayed in their enormous house and played video games, and drove whenever they wanted to go anywhere. And with her other cousins, who lived on a farm in Nebraska, she could walk for miles through the cornfields.

Life was so different everywhere. Everyone had their own path, their own story. And here she was in hers, turning pages. Moving through the chapters, one at a time.

There was a rustle to her left. Could it be the squirrels? She turned down the light, watching for little scurrying shadows along the side of the tent before she realized it was just Wren getting comfortable.

"Are you still awake?" Amber whispered.

"Yeah," came the reply. "It's cold. Do you think they'll come?"

"I dunno," Amber said. "Maybe it's good if they don't."

"What do you mean?"

"Well, we just want the destruction to stop, right? If it really is squirrels, what would we do except scare them away? As long as the projects are safe long enough for us to finish them, I don't care who is messing up the stuff. I'd be happy if they just never came back."

Wren rolled over to face the other side of the tent. Amber could see the ready light from Wren's camera disappear as her shoulder eclipsed it from view. Wren was determined to get photographic proof and sell the images to a newspaper for enough money to fix the microscope.

"Squirrels always come back," Wren mumbled. "They're survivors, even the ones that aren't zombies. And raccoons. They live in the sewers and climb out at night. I hope it's not a zombie raccoon though. Those critters can get mean."

Wild animals, bugs, and birds lived all around them, hidden and thriving despite all the concrete and the pest control and the tree grooming. Despite humans moving in and taking over entire habitats. So much wildlife lived even here amidst the bars and cable cars. Even heroic little sprouts poking up through the cracks in the sidewalk and worms feasting on the soil beneath.

"Nature always finds a way," Amber whispered.

33

MOVING ON

*S*omething scratched at the tent door. Amber bolted upright, completely awake, and nudged Wren. Wren let out a high pitched whine and pulled the top of her sleeping bag over her head.

The morning sun lit up the entire tent. The shadow on its door was clearly not a zombie squirrel.

It was Wren's dad.

"Hey, girls," he called. "Knock knock. I brought you some hot chocolate."

Unzipping the flap, Amber took the steaming mug. "Yum, thanks!"

A glance at the Greenhouse told her no one had attacked it last night. The door was still latched.

"Did you have fun?" Wren's dad asked. "Warm enough?"

"Yeah, but it was colder than I thought." Amber sipped

at the mug of sweet chocolatey goodness. "Thank goodness for warm jammies."

He laughed. "Wren still zonked?"

"Oh yeah," Amber smiled.

"I'm gonna let you wake her up." Wren's dad handed her the second steaming mug. "The price of hot chocolate delivery."

With a wink, he turned back to the house as Amber nudged the sleeping mound beside her.

"Whaaaaat?" Wren moaned. She batted at the offending hand. Then, smelling chocolate, she pried open an eyelid. She sat up and reached for the warm mug. "Oh. Oh, I like that."

As Wren slurped down her hot morning beverage, Amber lifted the flap of the tent again.

"Look," she pointed. "The tape you wrapped around the Greenhouse latch is still there, and see through the window? The stuff hasn't been touched. Nothing came to mess it up last night after all."

"Cowards! They're too scared of us to show up. But I wish we'd gotten proof." Wren dug in her sleeping bag for the camera. "My battery's dead anyway."

Wren led them inside for a Saturday morning breakfast. Amber assumed the Sterlings were getting sick of her by now. She felt like their third child these days. But they continued to welcome her warmly in the tiny, packed house.

After Wren's dad made them each a lovely bowl of oatmeal, they were ready to get back to work. Kammie's outfit was finished. Amber had rinsed the dyed pieces and threw them in the dryer at home, then assembled them. The beets and turmeric were her favorites, and the berries resulted in a lovely soft blue. Gentle and sophisticated, just like Kammie. The green hadn't turned out very well though.

The completed outfit now hung safely in her closet. Ivy's was done too, including the light-up purse. Bright LEDs nestled in fabric flowers, sewn onto the front purse flap. The conductive thread connected the snaps to the LEDs and batteries, completing the circuit when the flap closed.

Everything was coming together. Assuming the squirrels really were done with their rampage, they might just finish in time despite all the setbacks.

The last remaining hurdle was the smallest. Or at least the shortest. Trixie.

After making sure everything was set up in the Greenhouse, Amber checked in that Wren had everything she needed to get started. Wren nodded and began to work on her own outfit. Ivy hadn't arrived yet, so she finally had time to find out what was going on. Amber told Wren she'd be back, and headed to the house to find Trixie.

"Hey there." Amber gently cracked open the door to the girls' shared bedroom.

Trixie, knitting diligently on her chain, looked up from inside a pile of stuffed animals. As soon as she saw Amber, she began to cry.

"What is it?" Amber pushed aside the two hundred and

forty-three stuffed animals and squeezed next to her on the bed. "Talk to me."

"No," Trixie folded her arms and looked away.

"I've been trying to figure out what's wrong. What happened to my little Renegade? Why aren't you out there helping?" Amber pleaded. Then a horrible thought struck her. "Did somebody hurt you, Trixie?"

Trixie's eyes filled with tears. "Yes," she whispered.

"Oh my gosh!" Cold fear washed over Amber. "Who? Who hurt you?"

"You did."

Amber blinked. "What?"

"I don't want you to go away."

"Go away?" Amber's head spun. "Where would I go?"

"When you win the contest, you won't come over anymore. You said so." Tears and snot oozed from Trixie's squinched face. Her back began to shudder as she started to sob. She covered her face with her yarn-covered hands and continued to cry in a flood of held-back emotion.

"What? What are you talking about? Is that why you haven't been coming out?" Amber's stomach churned. This was her fault? "Where did you get that idea?"

Trixie leaned toward her. Amber wrapped her in her arms and rocked them both back and forth. She vaguely remembered saying something about being too busy for the club if she won. It had been a casual joke. She hadn't even considered Trixie might misunderstand. But all Trixie wanted from Amber was to be special to her. She should have known, should have seen.

Amber squeezed Trixie harder. "If I win, which I probably won't, I'll still see you all the time. Maybe even more."

"Really? You won't go away?" Trixie wiped her snot on Amber's shirt.

"I promise." Amber looked around for a tissue. "Look, I really need your help. Your outfit is the most important one in my entire collection! Can you help me? Be my most important fashion model? Trixie, you're really important to me. I want you to be part of everything."

With pink puffy eyes and snot dripping from her nose, Trixie stopped crying. Just like that.

"I sure can!" she nodded. "Look! Look at my yarn! I've been working on it just like you said. It's going to help, right?"

Oh yeah. Amber forgot she'd told Trixie her finger knitting would be important. She'd only meant to keep her busy, but now Amber would fit it in somewhere special. Trixie hadn't let her down, and she wasn't going to let Trixie down.

"Oh yes," Amber told her. "It's an important part of the show. Keep it safe! We can't let the squirrels ruin it!"

"Don't worry," Trixie laughed, "I won't ruin my own thing!"

She stopped and looked up with wide, guilty eyes.

"What?" Everything clicked into place. Trixie. Trixie was the zombie squirrel. She was the one destroying everything. Trixie who loved her enough to be mad at the idea of losing her. "Why? Why would you do that to me?"

"I want things to stay the same," Trixie squirmed. "If you don't get the thing, you won't leave."

Amber looked down at her, expecting to feel the familiar warm rush of anger. Expecting to have to take deep breaths. But the anger didn't come. Amber felt frustrated, absolutely. Annoyed. But not angry.

She understood what Trixie was feeling. This wasn't about Amber and her own hopes to be someone special, this was about a scared little girl who loved her.

"Hmmm," Amber struggled to find the right words. "You know what I've been realizing? What we want isn't always the right choice. Everything changes. What we want has to change too. We can't change the choices we made or the harm they've done, we can only try to make it better. We can make today good. We can choose to do the right thing, right here, right now. I didn't realize how much what I do affects other people. You probably didn't either. You didn't realize the consequences to the rest of us when you destroyed our stuff."

"Uh," Trixie hesitated. "Does that mean you won't tell anyone?"

Amber shook her head. "I'll make you a deal. You come back and help, and I won't tell anyone. I'm just glad we can finish up without worrying about more zombie squirrel attacks."

34

DRESSING ROOM FIVE

The night of the Fashion Face-Off was dark and cold, but Amber was sweating. She wiped her palms against her skirt before grabbing the door handle to Bespoke.

Warmth and light poured out of the glittering store into the cold December night outside. Amber led everyone in. She'd only been allowed to bring her own family as guests. She'd assigned Aiden a job for her presentation. Even though both her brothers were annoying, she knew they'd cheer for her. And she knew how loud they could be. She'd never tell them so, but she was glad they were there.

Clothing racks lined the sides of the store, clearing the way for a wide red carpet that stretched from the carpeted stage built across the entryway all the way to the back of the store, where a giant curtain stretched from wall to wall across the dressing room area. Rows of folding chairs facing the raised stage surrounded the aisle on both sides. They walked up the single step onto the stage, then back down another step to get into the store on the other side.

Wren jumped up, ignoring the step, and stomped on the stage, listening to its hollow thump before vaulting over the other step to land on the carpeted aisle. Ivy strode forward confidently, with Kammie following closely behind. Trixie wove around and between them, darting through the crowd like a colorful little fish. They passed through the audience on their way to the dressing rooms. Amber's breath came quicker with each step.

The rows of folding chairs were half empty. Half full. She wasn't sure if she was feeling optimistic or pessimistic. Several of the people already seated watched her group, trying to figure out which one was the designer. Amber heard a few mumbling about how young she was.

Suddenly Amber stopped dead in her tracks. Blaise bumped into her back.

"Hey," he whined. "Move it!"

"Sorry," she whispered, rooted in place. The unmistakable top of Milo Jones' head was four chairs from the aisle, three rows back. She could almost smell him. As Blaise shoved past her, Amber turned to Wren, whispering. "Is that *MILO*? What's he doing here?"

"Oh, hey Milo!" Wren waved, calling over the noise of the crowd. Amber shhhushed frantically, hiding her face.

Too late.

Milo, looking bored, glanced up at the sound of his

name. He stood and stretched, waving enthusiastically at them. The loose sleeves of his gray linen shirt fell back from his wrists as he lifted them above his dark, wavy hair. He had on fancy well-tailored navy slacks under the casually untucked shirt. His deep chestnut eyes sparkled as they approached.

Amber shook her head vigorously to clear it. With a deep breath she practiced saying hello, a skill she tended to forget around Milo.

"Hey there," he said to Wren. "What are you doing here?"

"I could ask you the same thing, weirdo," Wren teased him. "Since when are you a fashion designer?"

"Nah," Milo laughed. "It's my brother. The older one. I'm just here to support him. He's a great artist but not very confident. I had to come with him to drop the application off too."

Wren tossed her hair dramatically. "Well I'M a fashion model for Amber, here."

"Oh, hi Amber," Milo smiled meltingly. "I didn't see you there. You're in the competition? That's awesome! You look nice."

Amber looked down at her feet and blushed to the tips of her ears.

"She's been working really hard. Her collection is AMAZING. But we have to go, don't we?" Wren tugged on Amber's arm as everyone else from their group disappeared behind the back curtain. "See you later."

Trixie's head popped out, looking for them. Amber

waved back in Milo's direction while Wren dragged her away. As they joined the rest of their group behind the curtain, Amber caught a glimpse of blue hair in the direction of the audience.

"Hey," she said, "isn't that Jewels?"

Then, as the curtain closed behind her, she forgot everything else.

Swarms of kids, at least four or five years older, were throwing around clothes and sheets of paper with colorful illustrations on them. Their loud voices blended together in a droning hum. Ivy chatted with a tall woman who had a clipboard and an earbud. Kammie stood close to Ivy, looking around at the other kids and hugging the bag of fashions tightly to her chest.

Ivy nodded to the woman, waving to Amber. "We're in dressing room five," she called.

Amber turned to her parents and brothers. "I think you're supposed to go sit out there."

Amber's mom beamed down at her. She wrapped Amber up in a hug so big it lifted her off the floor. Her coconut and orange smell enveloped Amber as she whispered, "Knock 'em dead, sweetie."

"Moooom!" Amber looked around at the other contestants with a scandalized expression. No one else seemed to notice, though one boy pushed past them frantically. Amber remembered seeing him that first day in Bespoke, the boy wearing eyeliner.

"Let's go find seats before she dies of embarrassment,"

Amber's mom laughed as she clicked out of the curtained area on her high heels. Her dad shook her hand in a serious, businesslike way before following.

Amber hefted her backpack full of papers and shoved her way through to dressing room five.

35

JEWELS

"You guys look amazing," Amber gushed. Ivy, Kammie, Wren, and Trixie stood in a row in front of her. All of them in her designs. Designs she'd dreamt up and, with their help, constructed with her own hands. The full-length mirrors of the dressing room reflected all five of them, standing together. Together.

Amber admired herself. Her short auburn hair gleamed in the flattering dressing room light, embedded with rhinestones she'd picked off a shirt and glued to hair clips and bobby pins. Her hair looked artfully disheveled but had actually taken at least twenty minutes to style. She loved the way it looked unruly in just the right way.

Her mom let her wear lipstick tonight, a color that matched her hair. Sapphire rhinestones glittered in her ears and at her throat, gems pirated off the same shirt that supplied the sparkles for her hair.

Her dress was a matching sapphire blue. A satiny tank top, well loved but discarded for the crime of being too small, now fit perfectly again thanks to a creamy strip of new velvet fabric added to the front and back from another outgrown shirt. Black t-shirt yarn laced up the front across the velvet strip, looking like a cross between a princess's bodice and a sneaker. Sewn to the bottom of the bodice, wide strips of various blues shimmered and swung against her legs, making the skirt of the dress. The strips were all wider at the bottom, allowing the skirt to flare out with every step she made. The soft blue fabrics felt like puffs of air as they swept around her legs.

Beneath it all, over heavy wool tights dyed a gentle purpley-blue, her oxblood Doc Marten boots sported sapphire laces, made from a blue t-shirt.

Over Amber's shoulder, containing her notes and presentation materials, lay a soft pink cotton bag. Once upon a time, the bag had been a favorite t-shirt, pink glitter forming swirls around the word "Princess." She'd sewn the bottom closed, cut out the sleeves and sewn in a bit of ribbon at the shoulder to make the straps longer. The shirt's flowery word sat smack dab front and center of the bag. She'd embraced the word and made it her own.

Feeling like a sparkling rag doll princess, she loved every inch of her reflection. She couldn't love it more. Whoever she was now, this look felt right. It felt like the real her, and if the judges didn't like it, well, that wasn't her concern. But she did care what one person out there thought.

"Are you okay waiting here?" Amber asked the others as she opened the dressing room door. "Looks like we're presenting last. But before things get started, I wanted to go talk to someone."

"Oh heck yeah," Wren seemed relieved. "It's too loud and weird out there."

Kammie nodded enthusiastically.

"You go on," Ivy waved her out the door. "I'll take care of these two."

Out in the melee, Amber scanned the top of the crowd for blue spikey hair. But no blue surfaced through the waves of people around her.

Someone bumped into her and barked something rude. The girl was blonde, maybe sixteen, with hair pulled back into a massively long braid over her dark orange...was it a kaftan? A giant poncho-like dress.

"Hey," Amber asked, "have you seen a woman with blue hair running around?"

"Who, Juliana?" The girl rolled her eyes. "You won't be able to pin her down."

The girl pulled open the door to dressing room three and yelled something at the two kids inside. They both yelled back.

Amber poked her head through the curtain and gasped.

People packed the seats in the audience. So many people! Babbling, waiting, reading what looked like a program. They were all waiting to stare at the contestants. Judge them. Decide their worthiness. Four empty seats near the stage each held nothing but a clipboard, a pen, and a sign that said "Reserved for judges."

Off to the side of the stage sat a large whiteboard on wheels. A grid drawn on it listed five names down the left side: Raven, Marcus, Andrea, Siobhan, Amber. Along the top, it was divided into five categories: style, originality, craft, presentation, and, finally, total score.

Near the judges' seats, talking with the young man who'd taken over for her at the counter at Bygone, stood Jewels. Amber stepped outside the curtain, but Jewels was already heading back to the dressing area, surrounded by people asking her questions. Amber scooted back inside just as Jewels came through the curtain.

"You're here!" Amber cried, smiling. "It's so good to see a friendly face!"

"Of course I'm here." The blue-haired woman stopped, motioning her entourage away as she looked down at Amber. "It would be hard to judge the Face-Off if I were home on my couch!"

"I didn't know you were a judge," Amber giggled. "That's cool."

"Oh, right, I forgot," Jewels smirked. "There's a lot you don't know about me, Amber Rosenberg. But I suspect it's mutual."

Amber caught sight of the girl in the orange kaftan dress glowering at her as she talked with Jewels. Amber waved pleasantly at her. The orange girl huffed back into her dressing room.

"So, you ready to win?" Jewels asked.

"Nah," Amber said. "I won't win. But I sure am ready to show off."

"Niiiice," Jewels laughed. "Look, I'm pretty busy, but good luck. Oh, some young reporter girl out there was asking about you. Gotta run!" And the crowd immediately swallowed her up.

Reporter?

Amber stuck her head back out of the curtain. Sure enough, Gail Mendez, her eighth-grade friend, was clicking away with her phone's camera. Amber had met Gail during the student elections, but hadn't spoken to her or Benjamin Spencer in over a month. The sixth grade and eighth grade classes were on different floors of the school, and the eighth graders tended to eat lunch on the rooftop deck, so it wasn't too strange they hadn't run into each other, but still. Amber had resigned herself to the idea that Gail and Ben had forgotten about her. But Gail waved at her eagerly, running over.

"There you are, Amber!" Gail panted. "I heard you were a contestant..." she gasped. "Oh my god, I LOVE your hair! Wait, tell me you didn't just cut it for this competition? Because THAT would be dedication."

"No," Amber laughed. "I cut it a few weeks ago."

"Oh," Gail cringed. "Sorry, I've been really busy with midterms coming up and getting ready for high school. Ben and I were talking about you guys just the other day, wondering how you all were doing. Sorry we haven't been around lately. It gets really crazy at the end of middle school. High school is truly intimidating."

"I can't imagine anything intimidating you, Gail," Amber stared at her doubtfully.

Gail gave her a sideways grin. "Everybody has something that scares them. Anyway, good luck. I'm covering the Fashion Face-Off for the *Gazette*. Look, I got a special press pass! Ben says to tell you good luck, and if anybody can do it, you can."

That was unexpected. Apparently she had more friends than she thought. Maybe she didn't only impact people in negative ways. Or maybe she'd just adapted well. Maybe, she, like nature, always found a way.

Up at the judges' seats, Jewels rang a loud gong.

"Oh!" Amber cried. "We're getting started! I gotta go."

She pulled her head back behind the curtain, paused, then stuck it out again.

"Thanks!" she called after Gail, who gave her a thumbs-up as she moved to a better vantage point of the stage.

"Okay," Amber said out loud, rubbing her hands together. "It's showtime."

She looked around for a place to watch the action before it was her turn. She might be in the competition, but that was no excuse to miss it!

Upcycled Bag

Materials:
Old t-shirt
Scissors

Optional:
Ribbon or fabric scraps
Hand sewing tools or
Sewing machine

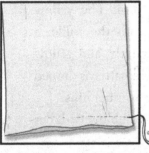

Cut off collar in a big
scoop shape

Cut off
sleeves

Cut a little longer than
you want the final bag

Turn the shirt inside
out and stitch along
the bottom or seal it
with duct tape.
Tug on the straps, turn
your bag right side out,
and it's DONE!

Tips:

Fold and stitch the raw edges... or don't. Whatever!
If the straps are too short, snip at the shoulder and
sew in an equal length of ribbon or scrap fabric on
each side (maybe use the sleeves or shirt bottom?)

36

SHOWTIME

*R*aven went first. She was a short girl of maybe 15 with rope-like black braids wrapped around her head, knotted in the back. A bright yellow ruffle draped elegantly across one of her dark shoulders at an angle, wrapping beneath her other arm. The yellow highlighted her skin's dark tones. Beneath the ruffle, a patchwork of brightly colored blue, burgundy, and yellow fabric tucked tightly at her waist. The bold patterns draped and flared from her waist, drifting gently over her hips.

She approached the stage nervously, fumbling with her notes.

"Hello," she began in a rich, loud voice, "My name is Raven. Thank you for letting me share my collection with you today."

Thanking the audience upfront! Great idea! Amber quickly scribbled a greeting into her notes. All the other contestants were watching from the edges of the curtains, too, but none of them took notes. Eyeliner boy, on the other side of the room, took a few deep breaths, though. His profile looked familiar, but Amber had no idea where she would have met him, besides seeing him briefly in Bespoke. He seemed almost like someone she knew. Next to her, the girl in the huge orange dress looked right over Amber's head.

Raven continued, pulling out various drawings and fabric swatches. Her inspiration came from mixing the kente fabric from her father's side of the family, and the Scottish plaids from her mother's. She explained how both types of fabric were bound to identity. How each set of colors and patterns in both tartan plaids and kente cloth represented various clans or tribes. Through time and colonization, many of those identities had been lost, with many of the patterns from both fabrics now used more as a novelty. Entire familial identities bought and sold for their beauty. She'd done her research on her own rather unusual legacy from both Ghana and Scotland, and mixed her own ancestral fabrics to become the foundation of her collection.

Three kids came out, all teenagers. Two girls and a boy, wearing modern formal clothing made with a blend of plaids and African prints. Amber was amazed at how Raven had been able to blend colors and patterns that didn't seem to mix at all. The subtle grays and navy blues of the tartans created backdrops for bright oranges and greens. The boy wore a kilt made from kente cloth with traditional Scottish long socks under a tuxedo tailcoat with a tartan pocket square and tie. One girl wore a royal blue satin dress that swept gracefully behind her with a scarf in yellow, orange, and a perfectly matching blue.

Raven and her models left the stage to thunderous applause. Raven, however, looked like she might faint. Amber caught her eye and sent her a warm smile and two thumbs up. Raven nodded appreciatively, flopping into an empty seat. The boy model wrapped his arms around her as she leaned on his shoulder.

From the front, Amber heard Jewels call out "Next, please welcome MARCUS JONES!"

Jones! The pieces fell together. Eyeliner boy was Milo's brother! That's why his profile looked familiar. Across the room, he smoothed his bleached hair and knocked on the door of dressing room two.

Four kids, ranging in age from probably eight to maybe eighteen, filed out. Two boys and two girls. They all had the same warm brown skin and long, sleek, black hair. They all had Milo's same lovely brown eyes. Why wasn't Milo with them?

Their outfits were simply breathtaking. Modern sleek lines blended with Victorian curves. Velvets in black and jewel tones, feathers in their hair, collars that defied gravity, and they all wore little Victorian booties with kitten heels, even Marcus himself. Amber's jaw dropped.

Marcus took a deep breath and led the way through the curtain. Before they'd even made it to the front, the audience burst into applause. The girl in orange muttered a curse word.

"I have to follow that?" she mumbled. "Crap."

She must be Andrea, Amber thought, trying to remember all the names. Or was it Abigail? Everything was starting to blur together. She tried not to panic.

Her confidence wavered. She knew she had no chance to win, but she didn't want to humiliate herself, or the other Renegades. These other kids were SO GOOD.

But also, Amber realized, a lot older too. What could she be in four or five years if she kept at it? Just last year she could never have imagined being in this room at all.

Andrea's collection looked like a sunrise; orange, yellow, pink, and bright plummy purple with hints of turquoise blue. Her models were older than she was, and she must have been at least sixteen. They all had model-like bored pouts as well.

Andrea seemed to really like long, floaty fabric. All her fashions sported layers and layers of them. The models spun around frequently as she tossed out fabric swatches and talked about feeling like floating on air and being in the sunrise of her fashion career. It seemed a bit self-indulgent to Amber, but watching the colors swirl and blend really did fill her with a kind of hope. It felt fresh and new.

Jewels called out the fourth designer, pronouncing Siobhan "Shi-vawn." Emerging from the fourth dressing room with her models, Siobhan had even shorter hair than Amber's. Intense green eyes were framed in thick purple eyeliner. Amber had no idea how old she was. Both her models were boys. They and Siobhan all wore cloaks, pulling up the hoods simultaneously as they glided through the curtains and down the red carpet. They moved so smoothly they looked like floating black specters.

Amber didn't stick around long enough to see what was under the cloaks. The back area was empty now, since the contestants and their models sat in the few remaining audience seats after their presentations. Although going last gave her time to scope out the competition, it also gave her time to get really nervous. Now she knew how hopelessly outclassed she was. But again, it didn't matter, right? She was here to spread a message. Right?

Applause broke out from the audience side of the curtain. Siobhan's group must have taken off their cloaks.

Amber opened the door of dressing room five. It was her turn.

37

AMBER'S TURN

On the stage at the end of the red carpet, Amber looked out at fifty people staring back at her.

"I'm Amber Rosenberg," she said in a surprisingly strong, clear voice. "Thank you for letting me share my fashions with you." She winced, realizing that was almost exactly what Raven had said. Whoops. Move on, move on. She looked up from her notes for a moment and spoke from her heart instead. "Honestly, I'm not sure how I got to be up here with these amazingly talented designers. Seriously, you guys are incredible. I hope to someday be as inspiring as you. So thanks for letting me be a part of this. And I hope you listen to what I have to say. Because it's important, beyond me, beyond this competition."

She took a deep breath and turned back to her notes. "Fashion. Fashion transforms us. Fashion empowers us. And today, fashion is destroying us. What we do matters. Our choices, big and small, matter. Our choice of style, down to the smallest detail, defines us. All my life, people have assumed a pretty dress meant an empty head. That a girl can only be one thing: smart or pretty. That liking makeup or unicorns or boys automatically means a girl can't also like school, or science, or building things. And honestly, that's just stupid. When other people think that way, it doesn't mean I'm stupid, it means they're the stupid ones."

Several people in the audience fidgeted or laughed uncomfortably. Amber faltered, but found her place in her notes again. Sometimes the truth can make people uncomfortable, but that was okay. *It's only your job to speak truthfully*, she told herself. *It's their job to listen or not*. But maybe she could reframe the idea in a more positive way so they'd be able to listen better. "A scientist can wear whatever she wants, whether it's cargo pants or a pencil skirt. As long as it has pockets."

A louder, more genuine laugh rewarded her. Amber was shocked at how important it felt to get their approval. People she didn't even know, in a contest she kept telling herself she didn't really care about. But then, she wasn't a complete jerk. Of course it mattered to her what other people thought. She just couldn't let it control her.

"The noun *fashion* means a trend, a style of clothing," she continued. "But the verb *fashion* means to make into a particular form. Fashion can be a passive word or an active word. Active fashion is what we're here for tonight. The act of fashion.

"I'm here to show people that what's on my body does not limit what's in my head."

More applause. She glanced up at the audience with a new wave of nerves. Okay, this was it. Time to get serious. She flipped to her next note card.

"But the fashion industry is destroying our world. It's one of the world's greatest polluters, and most people don't even know it. While preparing for this event, I've learned the truth about the damage the clothing I love causes the Earth I also love. That knowledge has made me want to change. I want to share these two important journeys with you now. One is finding a way to blend what's in my head and heart with what's on my body, and the other is doing that while causing the least amount of damage to the planet as possible. It's hard to hear, hard to change, but it might be the most important thing ever. Knowledge has changed me, and I hope what I'm going to tell you will change you too."

She glanced over the top of her note cards, but couldn't read the expressions in the audience. Had she just made them all angry? Curious? Bored? No way to know.

"I hope you like my collection," she persisted.

And she hoped Aiden would do his job. Out in the audience, his head bobbed through the aisles heading for the outside wall. He wasn't clear of the seats yet. She motioned desperately for him to hurry up. If he didn't reach his destination in time, Ivy's outfit would be a disaster. Trusting him was her only option, so she took the leap and continued.

"Science is powerful!" Ivy stepped from behind the curtain, striding down the red carpet. Her sleek black hair swung from a high, tight ponytail as she walked, skimming her shoulders and showing off ruby-colored earrings. She wore a loose red shirt. They'd pieced together the fabric from Ivy's outgrown soccer uniforms. After all the setbacks, Amber hadn't had time to construct a proper armhole and shoulder seam, so she'd adapted and opted for stylish batwing sleeves, like a fitted poncho. A square of fabric angled and sewn on the sides, without defined sleeves at all. A dark grey sash wrapped in a wide swath around her hips, cinching the fabric smoothly, leaving several inches of the shirt to dangle halfway down her thighs.

Grey leggings peeked out from under the shirt. They had once been a pair of too-tight sweatpants. Ivy had been the hardest Renegade to fit, being both older and naturally tall and broad. So again, Amber adapted. Instead of fighting to fit Ivy into a design, she'd created a design that fit Ivy. The sweats had been adjusted to be intentionally snug, the hems adorned with just a touch of rhinestone sparkle to bring the eye across the entire outfit. Ivy wore red flats, each adorned with a large fabric flower. The blue satin purse, slung across her body and over her shoulder by a double chain of finger knitting, bounced on her hip. The wild array of yarn colors and thicknesses in the strap looked playful against the simple color palette of the outfit, and drew in the colors of the three fabric flowers on the flap. The final outfit was both practical and business-elegant, with a few choice touches of glam.

At least Amber intended it to be practical and business-elegant. She had been so proud of how the outfit came together. But now it seemed childish and scrappy after the unbelievable outfits from the other designers. Seriously, what WAS she even doing here? An overwhelming urge to throw down her notes and walk out into the cold, dark night surged through her.

What was the point?

No. She'd brought her friends here. Her family. She couldn't abandon them. She might fail, she might even look like a fool, but she wouldn't let them down. This was her responsibility. Ivy was counting on her. She had to keep going. No one would save her except herself. If she wasn't a princess, then she'd be a queen.

By the time she looked at her notes again, Ivy was already halfway down the aisle.

"Ivy," she squeaked, then coughed to clear her throat. "Ivy is dressed for another day running a company, blending the power of an athlete with her powerful will to succeed. This elegant outfit is made from upcycled athletic clothes. The synthetic fabric wicks sweat away from the body, so even if you're going on a special date after work, you won't sweat through your clothes!"

Amber loved the joke. Ivy hadn't liked it, though, and apparently she was right. No one laughed. Amber sighed. This was not going well. Ivy climbed up the stage and stood next to her, head held high.

"Her earrings are made from bio-plastic created with milk. Scientific knowledge lets you make things you never knew you could. Science even lets us harness the power of light itself!" Ivy connected the metal snaps on the purse with an audible click, turning to point the purse at the audience. Nothing happened.

The LEDs were invisible in the bright light of the store. Amber looked around frantically for Aiden. He'd pushed his way through to the light switches just a few seconds late and slammed his palm against them now.

The crystal chandeliers went dark.

The audience gasped.

Ivy's purse lit up, sparkling with bright colors. The fabric the flowers were made out of glowed too, increasing the effect. The flowers on her shoes were rigged with LEDs as well. With no way to put in a switch, they'd attached the batteries in the dressing room. The shoe lights had been on the whole time, invisible in the store lights. Now in the dark, they glowed beautifully.

Ivy twirled around to the oohs and ahhs of the crowd. That positive feedback had an oversized impact on Amber's confidence. By the time Aiden flipped the lights back on, Amber's voice called out loud and clear again.

"Science is colorful!" she said, and Kammie, looking down at the carpet, her face a bright pink, stepped from the curtain. "Toxic chemicals from fabric dyes pollute the water systems of the Earth. So we found a way to protect our oceans and rivers without dulling our statements. Natural dyes may not be as vibrant and showy as chemical dyes, but it's that very subtlety that creates the most special kind of beauty. A beauty that doesn't overwhelm you. It invites you to come find it and all its secrets. Kammie wears an upcycled outfit of natural fibers colored entirely by vegetables, plants, and water. Done the right way, fashion can be transformative and empowering."

At these words, Kammie lifted her head and stared straight at Ivy. She grew more confident with each step. With mid-length sleeves and simple lines, her outfit was styled after a salwar kameez, but instead of the traditional trousers, Kammie wore a skirt under the tunic. The sides of the soft cotton tunic were open from the hips down, which allowed it to go all the way down to her thighs without limiting her leg movement. The skirt underneath the tunic was a gathered silk, and hung to her mid-calf. The tunic was a strong, deep turmeric yellow that offset her warm brown skin beautifully. The color faded in an ombre towards the bottom. It had been a happy accident from moving the pots. The part of the fabric left in the dye longer was more colorful.

The colors blended beautifully from top to bottom. Deep yellow at her shoulders, fading to a lighter cream, over a gentle red of the beet-and-cranberry dyed longer skirt, and down to the red cabbage-colored leggings layered underneath the skirt, with subtle rhinestones glittering at their hems. Her shoes were deep purple Mary Janes, chosen more for their color than their style. She joined Ivy on stage.

"Science is creative!" Amber called loudly. Wren burst

through the curtain and strode down the carpet. More accurately, Wren skipped down the carpet. She stopped near Milo's row to spin around flamboyantly. Then she noticed Amber glowering at her and slowed down. Remembering she was a model, Wren stuck her lips out in a pout, thrust her nose in the air and continued with an exaggerated swing to her hips. Amber turned back to her notes, catching a glimpse of Milo applauding with a mischievous smile. He leaned into the aisle to watch Wren walk all the way to the stage.

Dark, woven t-shirt yarn encased Wren's body. The fat strands of black, navy, and the deepest, darkest purples wove in and out of each other at a diagonal in the front, a standard weave turned sideways like a diamond. It criss-crossed tightly over her torso. In the back, the yarn was knit together, hooking onto its own loops, connecting at the sides with the ends of the diamond weave. Once the strands reached her waist, they flowed freely, creating an active, flopping skirt that hung like the entrance to a car wash. Like a many-tentacled octopus dancing around her legs. It went all the way down past her knees. There were no sleeves on the dress; the yarn was woven tank-top style, with space between the strands to see the fabric under-neath. The wide weave allowed the dress to stretch enough to pull it over her head, so it didn't need zippers or buttons. The yarn was all dark or black colors.

Underneath the yarn, sourced from half a dozen gauzy and satin dresses, was a simple, bright yellow panel over her torso, and a skirt that swished dreamily around her legs in various yellows, mustards, and creams. The dark, strong, tight yarn almost looked like a cage, holding in sunny, exuberant fabric that flared and swished over her legs beneath the constant pounding and flopping of the yarn tendrils. A study in contrasts, the weave both held back the free-flowing skirt and supported the structure and interest of the entire piece. She looked like an exotic bird in a living cage.

Wren's feet were bare against the red carpet. Her ankle was bound in several looping strands of bio-plastic beads that matched the colors of her underdress. Her hair was unbound and wild around her exuberant face. She radiated in all the positive attention. She'd cut a shawl from the leftovers of one gauzy skirt, so it matched part of the dress's skirt perfectly. She flicked it sporadically behind her as she moved down the aisle, only wrapping it over her bare shoulders once she'd settled in next to Kammie onstage.

Finally Amber turned to the curtain and called, "SCIENCE IS OUR FUTURE!"

Trixie burst through the curtain, running toward the stage, looking around nervously.

"Walk!" Amber hissed at her. Trixie stared, frozen, at the crowd, who were laughing uproariously. Andrea, close to the front, snorted and looked towards Amber with a sneer. Trixie had on a tutu made of dozens of strips of tulle. The sheer fabric was secured to a strong elastic waistband. Above the skirt, Trixie wore one of Amber's old green satin shirts, virtually untouched.

"Trixie represents our future. What will we do with

our power to shape it? Trixie is wearing strips from torn clothes, old, new, heavily worn, and never worn. The kind of cast-off clothes that fill our landfills by the ton every month. The colors are earth shades, the Earth we all live on. Science is the past, present, and future of fashion. We have the power to control what we do with the knowledge it gives us."

Amber put down her notes.

"Thank you."

38

SILENCE

Silence.

No one moved. Amber stood at the front of the stage breathing as heavily as if she'd just run across town. She stood unmoving, her best friends behind her, facing a silent crowd. They stared back at her without a sound.

Defeat.

She waited for the crushing feeling of defeat to flatten her.

But, to her surprise, she actually didn't feel defeated, despite the silence from the crowd. She felt elated. Whether anyone heard her or not, she'd spoken her truth. To an audience. With a loud, clear voice. She'd done something very hard without quitting. Without giving up. She truly had done her best.

She felt proud and strong.

It didn't matter if no one praised her. She realized,

staring into the silent crowd, that it didn't really matter to her whether they liked what she said or not. Whether they believed she had a brain in her head or that her dress was nice. It really, truly, didn't matter.

Well, no, that wasn't entirely true. Deep in her heart, she knew, she did care what people thought of her. The thing now, the thing that had changed, was that she also cared what SHE thought of herself. That of all the opinions that mattered, her own was the most important.

Then, unexpectedly, someone started clapping. It wasn't even a polite clap, it was real. And it came from Milo.

Then her brothers clapped too. Her parents, embarrassed they hadn't started the whole clapping thing, began smacking their hands together as hard as they could. Then others, and others, and others. Real applause. Some people even stood up. Someone near the back whooped.

Even the judges joined in.

Looking over the crowd, she was surprised to see Marcus, sitting near Milo, standing and cheering. Raven and Siobhan applauded with enthusiasm too, and even sour-faced Andrea clapped briefly, reluctantly.

Amber curtsied to the crowd and the clapping got even louder. A force crashed into her from behind and she almost fell off the stage. The Renegades hugged her tightly. Ivy, Kammie, and Wren, with Trixie fighting to get inside the pile-up. Amber fought her arms free to hug them back.

"Thanks, guys," she whispered only loud enough for them to hear. "Thanks so much for everything."

"All YOU, boss!" Wren replied, booping her nose with a free hand.

Then, as the noise died down, they made their way to the only empty seats left. Milo's row had three, and there were two seats in front of those, almost as if he'd been saving them. Wren shoved Amber into the seat next to Milo and sat on her other side, fistbumping him over Amber's lap before she even realized what was happening. Ivy and Kammie sat together in the seats in front and Trixie balanced on her knees on the aisle chair next to Wren, fluffing out her tutu.

From all around them, cameras flashed repeatedly, reminding Amber of the paparazzi surrounding a movie premiere. She knew the flashes weren't just for the Renegades, but she pretended they were anyway.

Amber craned her head around, catching her mom's eye. Her mom blew her a kiss.

39

JUDGMENT

*M*urmurs and chatter filled the audience as the judges leaned their heads together. They held up their clipboards, discussing and pointing at them. Though everyone around her was talking, Amber felt like her head had been wrapped in plastic.

"Hey, Milo." Wren leaned over Amber again. "Your brother did a great job! Who were all those models?"

"My brothers and sisters," Milo shrugged.

"ALL of them?" Wren said with wide eyes. "Holy cats! That's a houseful!"

"Yeah, I know, right?" Milo agreed. "They're mostly okay, I guess. Miranda can be a pain in the butt."

"Well, why weren't you out there with them, all fanci-fied?" Wren still talked over Amber, who was trying to decide between staring straight ahead and ping-ponging her head back and forth as they spoke.

Milo pointed to his foot and tried to lift it so they could

see. It was in a big yellow brace. "Sprained my ankle trying to walk in those tiny heels. I was going to do it anyway, wearing this clunky thing, but Marcus said the lines were wrong or something. Didn't go with the look."

Wren laughed but Amber looked scandalized.

"That must have totally destroyed his plan at the last minute!" She blurted, "Poor Marcus!"

Milo pointed meaningfully at his sprained ankle.

Amber blushed. "I mean, poor you too."

Thankfully, Jewels stood and rang her gong.

Silence blanketed the room immediately. All eyes turned to the blue-haired woman as she walked up onto the stage.

"They're letting Jewels announce the winner?" Amber mused out loud. "That's weird."

"Why?" Milo whispered. "She owns the store. Who else would it be?"

"SHE WHAT?" Amber yelled into the silence. A few heads flipped around to stare angrily at Amber. One of them shushed her urgently.

Amber didn't hear them. Jewels owned Bespoke? Then why was she working the counter at Bygone? No, there must be a mistake. Amber had never imagined a youngish woman with crazy hair would own such a well-designed store with such amazing fashions. She looked up on stage at the woman who was directing her fellow judges to place the whiteboard behind her. She'd just assumed Jewels was a random retail worker. Kind, smart, great sense of style, and all but...not the *OWNER* of BESPOKE. And here she was giving her cute little nicknames. Apparently, after all her anger about people underestimating her, Amber couldn't stop judging people either. It really was hard to see beyond the surface.

"Thank you all for coming," Jewels began. "I'm so impressed by the talent and creativity we've all seen here tonight. But..." She had to stop until the applause and whistling died down. "But there can be only one new youth intern at Bespoke. I know you're all anxious to hear the results, so we'll tally them here, now. You're all winners in my book, but one of you will leave today as part of my Bespoke family."

More applause. Ivy and Kammie cheered. Wren and Milo hooted and stomped. Between them, Amber clutched her hands together in her lap. She stared nervously at her blue-painted fingernails. Had Jewels seen them? Would she think Amber was trying to match her fingernails to her hair, she wondered frantically. That was just silly, but suddenly all her interactions with Jewels seemed suspicious. Did Jewels think Amber had been trying to manipulate her by asking advice?

Jewels continued as Amber watched her with embarrassment.

"The judges and I scored each contestant on a scale of one to ten for these four qualities," She pointed to the grid listing *Style, Originality, Craft, Presentation.* Then she pointed to *Total Score.* "The one with the highest score wins. Good luck to you all."

With that, she turned her back on the audience and

began copying numbers from a piece of paper in her hand. Amber watched breathlessly, only paying attention to the total scores as they were written.

Raven, twenty-eight. Marcus, thirty-two. Andrea, twenty-six. Siobhan, twenty-eight.

Her breath caught as she tried to add the numbers written next to her name. Style, six. Originality, eight. Craft, five. Presentation, six. Total Score, twenty-five.

Amber flopped down in her chair.

She'd lost. Last place. What did she expect? Some last-minute miracle? This contest wasn't a fairy tale, and she wasn't the princess. Marcus was the princess. Or, well, whatever. He was the hero of the story. Amber was just a side character.

Next to her, Milo stomped his heavy boot on the floor and yelled for his brother. He stood and high-fived the people in front of him. All around her, the crowd erupted into boiling chaos. People pushed through the aisles to hug each other.

Amber sat quietly in her seat, looking at her deep red boots, tears welling up in her eyes. Darn it! She wasn't supposed to care. She DIDN'T care, not really. It was just...

Arms wrapped comfortingly around her. With a ferocious wipe at her eyes, she sniffled. Wren's shoulder was there. She buried her face against the soft shawl, arms limp in her lap, barely conscious of the many hands patting her back and shoulders, or her parents calling to her, struggling to reach her through the melee.

"You did great," someone said. "It's okay."

She couldn't hear anything else above the din until she vaguely made out one voice trying to be heard. Then the gong sounded, loud and clear.

The hullabaloo died down. Amber felt a hand patting her back. She looked up and was surprised to see Milo smiling at her.

"You were incredible," he said.

Just then, Jewels' voice could finally be heard above the crowd.

"Hang on there, everybody!" she called. "I have some last-minute points to award."

40

BONUS

*L*ike ice water, the words shocked the entire room into silence. Everyone froze, looking at the stage.

"Don't worry, don't worry." Motioning for them all to sit down, Jewels smiled reassuringly. "The tally stands. I'm not a monster. The outcome hasn't changed. But I do want to make some last-minute adjustments."

Now even Amber was paying attention. Curiosity won out over her sadness.

"In the past few weeks, since opening Bygone a few doors down, I've learned some things about my own business. The fashion business that I've been in for over a decade. I opened Bespoke to offer something you can't get online. The big retail stores are dropping like flies and there isn't much room for innovation or creativity. Even mall stores, pumping out fashion faster than we can buy it, are closing their physical locations. So I wanted to start something with only unique designs. Only handmade, local items. One-of-a-kind, well made, keeper fashions, in hopes of bringing people back into the stores. Get them out of their living rooms and into the community. And so far, it's working. So I began to wonder how else I could provide a fashion service that would stop people from shopping entirely with their thumbs. To see and feel quality workmanship again. So I started Bygone, intending to offer well-priced, quality used items."

She paused, lost in her own thoughts. The crowd watched her silently.

"As people have been bringing in bag after bag of mall fashions," she continued. "I've really gotten to see how much waste is in our industry. And sitting here tonight, watching these promising young talents, up and comers in the fashion world all of you, one specific presentation has really made an impact. And I want to learn more. I want to do better."

Amber began to tingle.

"So," Jewels lifted her marker and turned back to the board. She squeezed in a fifth criteria column and wrote *Science* at the top. "I want to acknowledge one of our contestants who really did things differently."

As Amber watched, amazed, Jewels wrote a TEN in the *Science* column by her name. There was a huge uproar of applause and Amber hardly even noticed Milo, Milo of all people, giving her shoulders a quick squeeze. He said something Amber didn't register as she turned to look at him, but he smiled excitedly as he said it.

At the front, Jewels waited patiently. Soon, she raised her hands and the noise died down.

"We still have our Bespoke winner," she assured them. "Congratulations to Marcus Jones! I want you to join me up here in a minute. But our youngest competitor really dug deep against hard odds. Everyone should be so impressed with this young talent. Several weeks ago, when we were taking applications, I overheard her talking to her friends with such intelligence, such amazing knowledge of the science and engineering behind fashion, that I wanted to make sure she got a chance at the internship. I admit I was guilty of underestimating her based on her fancy and plentiful clothes at first. Now, after seeing her presentation, I've made a decision. As of this moment, I'm establishing a new youth internship at Bygone. Someone to help me create an Upcycling division and learn how my stores can become more sustainable. I need someone enthusiastic and knowledgeable to help me do better. And I can think of no one I'd rather work with on that than Miss Amber Rosenberg."

Cheers crashed through the crowd like a wave. People stood and turned to her as Amber's brothers, who had finally fought their way through, grabbed her arms and yanked her to her feet.

"Come on up here, both of you!" Jewels yelled above everybody.

Wren gave her a shove toward the aisle as her brothers practically dragged her down the carpet. Catching her in a hug from the sidelines, her mom got lipstick all over

Amber's face, showering her with kisses. Her dad messed up her hair, unable to stop ruffling it since he couldn't get in for a hug.

Near the front row, she met up with Marcus Jones, who gallantly offered her an arm. She took it and together, they climbed the steps to join Jewels on the stage. Jewels stood between them and grabbed each of their hands. Then, in a moment Amber would never forget, Jewels raised the hands together.

"Let's hear it for the winners!" Jewels yelled.

The crowd roared in approval.

41

THE END

Saturday afternoon sun streamed through the front windows of the Greenhouse, keeping the space warm and cozy. It wasn't quite Hanukkah yet, but the air was definitely cold. The winter rains were moving in. But not today.

Today was the perfect day.

Amber kicked her boots onto the top of the sturdy potting table and leaned back against the warm glass of the windows, lacing her fingers together behind her head. She looked around at her friends with an easy smile. They'd taken out the microscope and, despite the broken eyepiece, were arguing over who got to view the fibers first.

It was Amber's idea to check out the differences between silk, polyester, and cotton fabric, but she wasn't in any hurry to take her turn. She'd rather just enjoy the company.

"Oh, come on," Kammie pouted. "I never go first."

"You snooze, you lose!" Wren replied, putting her face to the microscope. "Huh, I did not expect that. Hey, Amber, check this out."

"Nah," she said. "It's Kammie's turn."

"Of course," Wren moved aside. "Here you go, Kammie. Hey, I just realized we haven't had any more attacks from the zombie squirrels."

"I don't think they'll give us any more trouble," Amber replied.

"Yeah," Wren nodded, watching Kammie adjust the microscope. "I bet we scared them away with the stakeout. Now that they know we're on to them, they won't show their bushy green little tails around here again. Zombie squirrels may not be smart, but they know when they've been defeated."

"Squirrels are gray, not green," Kammie corrected absently, not looking up from the eyepiece as she flipped on the backlight switch.

"Zombies, Kammie. Zombies are green. Not REGULAR squirrels for heaven's sake!" Wren threw up her hands. "Don't any of you people even watch movies?"

"You know what I'm interested in?" Ivy tugged at the bottom of her shirt. "I want to know HOW polyester wicks moisture away. I mean, it's hard to tell from just looking at it. I need more background research before I come up with a hypothesis and start experimenting."

"Let's put the polyester slide back on." Kammie reached for it.

"No!" Wren insisted. "Silk was next. I would think you,

of all people, would want to follow the order we already decided on."

They went back and forth until Ivy took both slides away and stuck the cotton one in place, pointing out something about its weave. Amber sighed happily and listened to them squabble.

Yes, perfect.

She'd start her new internship in January, and school was wrapping up for the holidays. She'd even found Axel and apologized. They'd both made mistakes, and they both deserved a second chance. Amber had even offered to take Axel on a behind-the-scenes tour of both Bespoke and Bygone. Maybe someday they might even be friends again.

There was nothing left to do for a while. Looking lazily over the inside of the Greenhouse, Amber saw the stuffed backpack she'd brought in the day she'd cut her hair. It was still unopened in the corner. She'd completely forgotten about it.

As if on cue, Trixie pushed open the Greenhouse door.

"Hi, can I come in?" she asked, coming in without waiting for a reply.

"Hey, Trix," Amber called from her comfortable perch by the windows. "Grab that backpack and bring it over."

Trixie brought it to Amber, then sat across from her.

"What's in it?" she poked at the backpack's soft sides.

"Just a little present for you," Amber winked. "I forgot to give it to you earlier. I hope you like it."

From out of the pack, Amber pulled dresses, shirts, skirts, and soft, delicate leggings. Pastel and jewel-toned hues mixed together like a liquid rainbow on the table as satins, tulle, and silks puddled where she dropped them. She even pulled out a pair of blue sequin-toed shoes. Trixie dipped her hands in the puddle of fabric, eyes wide with wonder.

"For me?" she looked up in amazement at Amber. "All of these?"

"Yup, my old absolute favorites, hand-picked just for you. Some of them might be a bit big. You might not fit in them all. Yet," Amber added, holding up a green sundress, "but I can't think of anyone who'd rock them better than you, little bug."

"Oh Amber!" Trixie cried. "Thank you!"

Trixie dropped the clothes and ran around the table, bumping into Ivy's back on the way around. She hurled herself into Amber's arm and cozied into a big hug.

"You're the BEST, Amber," she exclaimed happily, her eyes glittering. "When I grow up, I want to be just like you."

Amber rubbed Trixie's hair. "Well dressed and always stylish?" she asked playfully.

"Hopefully! And," Trixie looked her in the eye. "I want to change the world with science, too."

A

Acidic - scientists use the pH scale (potential for Hydrogen)to determine whether a substance is ACIDIC or ALKALINE/BASIC. The scale goes from 0-14, with 7 being neutral, not acidic or basic. Substances from 0-6 are considered acids, and ones from 8-14 are considered bases. Acids have a lot of hydrogen ions, and bases have a lot of hydroxide ions. Acids can break things down or corrode them.

B

Biodegradable - something capable of being decomposed (or broken down) into compounds that are easily absorbed into the soil to become nutrients or elements.

Biomass - a material made by plants and animals that can be converted into energy.

Bio-plastic - a plastic that is made from biological materials and can break down over time. However, these plastics need to be composted in large, industrial machines. They will not, for example, biodegrade in the ocean.

Buttonholing - making a buttonhole in a garment. Usually a buttonhole is made by sewing very small, tight, close stitches around the edges of a slit that is cut slightly smaller than the button that will go through it. These tight stitches act as a lining for the fabric and keep the edges from fraying or pulling apart.

Button batteries - also called coin cell batteries. Small, round, powerful batteries that look like buttons or quarters, commonly found in cameras, lights, car remotes, and other things. Button batteries can be dangerous if swallowed, so be careful with them!

C

Carbon footprint - the amount of greenhouse gases (specifically methane and carbon dioxide) that a person, industry, animal, or business releases into the environment by their energy needs. You can measure the carbon footprint of an item, like a backpack, or a company, like Apple, or a person, like yourself. It's used to get an idea of the pollution we create based on how we live.

Casein - a protein found in milk.

Cellophane - a thin, clear, crinkly plastic made from

cellulose (which is the main part of the cell walls of plants). It can't be recycled, but true cellophane is biodegradable, and can be composted.

Coalesce - to unite or clump together into one mass.

Coin cell batteries - the same as button batteries above

Conductive - able to transfer something like heat, electricity, or sound from one place to another. Metal is a good conductor, which means electricity can move easily through it. Plastic is a poor conductor (it's an insulator, which is the opposite of a conductor), so electricity doesn't move through it very well.

Conductive thread - sewing thread made out of fibers such as silver, copper, nickel, and stainless steel with a core of cotton or polyester. It carries electricity the same way a wire does, but is flexible enough to sew with.

Curdle - change to curds, to become lumpy, or separate into chunky bits. Similar to coalesce, curdle means clumping together. However, curdle usually means a liquid, like milk, clumps together in little chunks, so it goes from being a smooth liquid to being a bunch of lumpy chunks.

D

Deciduous - temporary or falling off. When used with plants, it means the type of tree or bush with leaves that fall off for part of the year.

Dip-dyed - a dyeing technique where the item is

dipped into a dye bath instead of being fully submerged. Usually that item is then pulled out very slowly, so the color is blended from the undyed area, to the brightly dyed part.

Diwali - the Indian festival of lights. It is one of India's largest festivals, taking its name from a row of clay lamps symbolizing the inner light protecting us from spiritual darkness. These pots are lit outside homes, in temples, and set to drift in rivers and streams. Diwali (also called Divali or Dipawali or Deepawali) is celebrated by people all over the world, including Hindus and Buddhists, and marks the new year. There are many wonderful traditions and interesting facts about Diwali, worth further research.

DNA - **D**eoxyribo**N**ucleic **A**cid is a molecule containing all the information about how a living thing will look and function. It's like a recipe with instructions our bodies follow as they develop.

E

Ecosystem - a community of all living and non-living things (like water, soil, and air) in an area and how they interact with each other.

F

Fast fashion - cheap clothes made very quickly in an effort to keep trends developing, in order to bring the latest fashion ideas to the consumer and keep people buying more and more clothes.

G

Genus and species - the way scientists group and classify living organisms, usually labeled with Latin names. Genus is a larger group that can include several species, grouped together by common traits. Species refers to sub-groupings.

Globalization - the exchange of things, people, ideas, culture, technologies, etc., around the planet. It is the connection of different parts of the world to each other through a chain of ideas, movement, and integration.

I

Insulate - to reduce the flow of electricity or heat energy. A non-conductive material that electricity can't move through, such as rubber, can be used as an insulator to keep the electricity moving only where it should go.

Interfacing - light, stiff fabric that is used to shape or reinforce a garment fabric. Interfacing is often used in collars to allow them to stand up or hold their shape.

Intern - someone who works in a temporary position to get some on-the-job training or insight into a career. Their work is not critical to the work an organization does; they mainly help people who do what they someday hope to do.

K

Keelhaul - a particularly dastardly form of pirate punishment. In practice, it just means getting in trouble, but for real pirates, it meant getting dragged down under the pirate ship and up the other side. Yikes!

L

Leads (electrical) - the wires coming out of an electrical device that allow electricity to enter and exit the device.

LED - stands for **L**ight **E**mitting **D**iode. A device that shines (emits) light.

M

Mai Oui - French for "but yes"

Microbiology - a branch of science that studies microscopic organisms, or, living things so tiny you can only see them with a microscope. These tiny living things include bacteria and viruses.

Microfibers - really tiny fibers that make up materials. It can mean the tiny fiber itself or the material made from it.

Millennia - thousands of years (plural for millennium - 1,000 years).

Molecule - the smallest bit of a thing that is still that thing. Scientists say it is the smallest unit of a substance that retains all the properties of that substance. A molecule is the smallest bit of water that is still water, but it is made up of even smaller parts: one oxygen atom and two hydrogen atoms

O

Oobleck - a substance made from cornstarch and water that has the qualities of both a solid and a liquid, but is neither. It is a non-Newtonian fluid.

P

Polarity - having two values. In electricity, it means the positive and negative charge, usually shown with a + or -.

Polymer - meaning 'many parts,' a polymer is a large molecule made of lots of little, repeating molecules called monomers. When monomers link together to form a polymer, it's called polymerization.

Proteins - a nutrient found in plants and animals. They build, maintain, and replace what bodies are made from such as muscles and organs.

S

Scalawag - a pirate insult meaning a person who is dishonest, or just a rascal.

Seam - the place where two pieces of fabric are sewn together.

Sewn circuit - a working electric circuit sewn onto fabric, usually using conductive thread.

Short (Electrical) - a short circuit is an electrical connection between two points electricity is not supposed to go directly between. They can be very dangerous.

Supply chain - a network of people and activities involved in moving a product from creation to consumer.

Synthetic - man-made, especially when made chemically, such as plastic.

T

Tesla - here, a really nice electric car. It's named after the brilliant scientist Nikola Tesla. Look him up, he's fascinating.

Textile - a woven or knitted cloth. Sometimes also meaning a yarn or fiber used to make cloth.

Trillion - a thousand billions. (Billion is a thousand millions, and a million is a thousand thousands.)

Tulle - a sheer (mostly see-through), light, thin cloth used for veils, some tutus, and evening or wedding dresses.

W

Wubby - for yarn, wubby means having a lumpy texture.

ACKNOWLEDGMENTS

There is no way to acknowledge everyone who contributes to a book. But as authors, we are compelled to do our best, because so many people help us in so many ways. I am so appreciative and deeply humbled for all the inspiration, help, and advice especially for a second book. I feel like it's natural to be excited about a first book, but the sequel is sort of the red-headed step-child. Or in Amber's case, the red-headed middle child. Hopefully my loved ones and supportive circle are not tired of my shenanigans and griping yet. 2020 has been an especially hard year to be creative. But with the wonderful support I've received, I've managed to produce something I'm really quite proud of.

With that in mind, I'd like to send loving thanks, in no particular order to:

My amazing husband who continues to bring me tea or wine, sometimes both, and believed in me and supports my efforts.

My son and daughter, without whom these books wouldn't even exist. Nor would they be anywhere near as readable. Thanks guys, I love you to the moon and back times infinity. Thanks for always believing in your silly mom, even when I'm annoying.

My Mom, who turned this book around with her insight. Once I finally got it through my thick skull what she was saying about my first few drafts, it made sense and was spot on.

All three of my sisters, women in STEM careers, inspiring young girls everywhere. And it's amazing how we all have been able to share home tips this year as we all settle into our various new digs.

To my nieces and nephews, I wish we could all spend more time together, but I love you more than you could possibly know. Because I so rarely tell you. Bad me.

My Dad, who couldn't be more supportive and Renee who weathers the storm with him.

My wonderful In-Laws, my belle-mère and beau-père, for their loving support.

To name a few names, thanks especially to:

Vicky for co-founding Renegade Girls, and being as vibrant and brilliant as you are hard-working. Briony for all her hard work for Renegades, and allowing me to use her wonderful family for research and inspiration. Juliana for writing dates, focus, oat milk chai, and friendship as well as letting me borrow inspiration from her kids and herself, and unknowingly letting me borrow her name. Solène, Audren, and Blaise for being such awesome inspiration.

My online friends, writing their own wonderful books and still taking the time to give me boosts of confidence. And Judeh for giving me camaraderie and the kick in the pants I needed at the right time.

And everyone else who has gone on this journey with me.

And I always want to thank the thousands of Renegade Girls and Boys who've shared their creativity, fun, and amazing tinkering prowess at the Renegade Tinkering summer camps and after school programs. You are the reason we exist, you are the future. Use your voices and brains and persistence to help each other and save the world!

ABOUT THE AUTHOR

Terri Selting David refused to believe that Colorado was "West", so she travelled more West until she couldn't get any West-er. San Francisco provided the perfect destination to pursue her love of technology, making stuff, art, and storytelling as a digital character animator. She spent over a decade making video games, film, television, and even a comic book. But tech wasn't always the most welcoming place for a woman, no matter how talented and passionate. Once her children came along, she was filled with a passion to make the world a better place for them, especially in the tech world.

So in 2015, she teamed up with her friend Vicky and founded the Renegade Girls Tinkering Club enrichment program to do what she could to make STEM a more welcoming place for the girls of the future. A few years later, she blended her background in storytelling, her digital skills, her art skills, and her experience writing curricula to write the Renegade Girls Tinkering Club novels, with a goal of bringing her projects to a wider audience and provide positive role models for girls facing the unique challenges of pursuing a love for technology, science, engineering, and math during a fragile time in everyone's life: middle school.

She lives in San Francisco with 2 rowdy children and a fabulous, brilliant husband who brings her tea every night.

ALSO BY TERRI SELTING DAVID

The Renegade Girls Tinkering Club:

Book 1 - The Renegade Spy Project

Book 2 - Renegade Style

--

Check out all the adventures of the Renegade Girls at:

www.RenegadeGirls.com

And visit Terri's author website at:

www.TerriSeltingDavid.com

CPSIA information can be obtained
at www.ICGtesting.com
Printed in the USA
LVHW041149260121
677519LV00002B/13

9 781735 454535